The Great Wheel

TEXT AND ILLUSTRATIONS BY

Robert Lawson

Foreword by Richard Peck

WALKER & COMPANY
NEW YORK

To
M.M.,
for whom
the little wheels run

This edition published in the United States of America in 2004
by Walker Publishing Company, Inc.

Published simultaneously in Canada by Fitzhenry and Whiteside, Markham, Ontario L3R 4T8

For information about permission to reproduce selections from this book, write to Permissions, Walker & Company,
104 Fifth Avenue, New York, New York 10011

Library of Congress Cataloging-in-Publication Data
Lawson, Robert, 1892–1957.
The great wheel / written and illustrated by Robert Lawson.
p. cm.
Originally published: New York : Viking Press, 1957.
Summary: Eighteen-year-old Conn leaves Ireland and sails to America, where he helps build the first Ferris wheel for the World's Columbian Exposition of 1893.
ISBN 0-8027-7392-3
[1. Ferris wheels—Fiction. 2. World's Columbian Exposition (1893 : Chicago, Ill.)—Fiction. 3. Emigration and immigration—Fiction. 4. Irish Americans—Fiction.] I. Title.
PZ7.L4384Gr 1993
[Fic]—dc20 92-19992
CIP
AC

ISBN 0-8027-7705-8 (paperback)

Visit Walker & Company's Web site at www.walkeryoungreaders.com

Printed in the United States of America

8 10 9 7

Walker Newbery editions you will want to read:

The Avion My Uncle Flew, Cyrus Fisher
Chúcaro: Wild Pony of the Pampas, Francis Kalnay
The Defender, Nicholas Kalashnikoff
Enchantress from the Stars, Sylvia Louise Engdahl
The Great Wheel, Robert Lawson
Kildee House, Rutherford Montgomery
Li Lun, Lad of Courage, Carolyn Treffinger
Mountain Born, Elizabeth Yates
The Moved-Outers, Florence Crannell Means
Old Ramon, Jack Schaefer
Swift Rivers, Cornelia Meigs

FOREWORD

In the middle of the twentieth century, in the last year of his life, Robert Lawson wrote and illustrated *The Great Wheel*. He was born the year before the wheel was, but in the way of a writer, he drew more upon other people's memories than his own. Many people in the 1950s still recalled riding history's first Ferris wheel at the great Chicago World's Fair of 1893. I remember those people myself, oldsters with misty-eyed memories of their first glimpses of the world from atop the mighty wheel.

Robert Lawson wove into the steel tracery of the wheel the story of an Irish immigrant boy, Cornelius—"Conn"—Kilroy, who helps to build it and get it going. But the book is in fact the biography of the first Ferris wheel.

It was the moon shot of its time, a great wheel 270 feet high, from the ground to apex, 1,700 tons of steel to lift thirty-six cabins the size of trolley cars—with velvet seats and floral carpets. *And* it cost four hundred thousand dollars to build. How much money that sum would represent today staggers the imagination. But more than money: would it get off the ground? No such mass had ever moved. Would it fall over and kill everybody involved? Would people who had never seen a building taller than a silo ride on the thing, even if they had the fifty-cent fare?

The answer is, naturally, yes. We are Americans. We're forever pushing the envelope and our luck. The whole idea for George Washington Gale Ferris's circular invention came of the American fair of 1893 trying to outdo the Eiffel Tower of the Paris exposition of 1889. Then as now the French were irritating us into action. What if we built a monument as steely and muscular as the Eiffel Tower . . . and it moved?

It's been said that the twentieth century began in Chicago at the World's Columbian Exposition. An electric century was foretold in this "White City," blazing brighter at midnight than at noon. The fairgrounds and the approach—the Midway Plaisance—now the campus of the University of Chicago, covered more than six hundred acres. It was threaded with gondola canals flowing from Lake Michigan: an ideal world of classical temples picked out in Edison's lightbulbs. Nothing could have that impact today. People fainted from the sheer grandeur and beauty of the fair.

But Robert Lawson saves his superlatives for the great wheel itself, and the unimaginable work of building it through an all-too-typical Chicago winter. For the foundations, sunk forty feet to hardpan, the concrete had to be mixed with live steam to keep it from freezing.

Who better to tell the tale than a broth of an Irish lad drawn mystically west to the New World, set upon his journey by a very Irish prophecy?

The building of the great fair is very much an immigrant experience:

> Micks, Squareheads, Polacks, and Dutchmen. A year or two now and they'll all be good Americans. A wonderful country is America, like a great stew pot, the way you can be throwing in all

them elements and it turning out a fine healthy dish. Barring a bit of scum, of course, that has to be whisked off. (pp. 14–15)

That's how Robert Lawson expressed it (in an Irish accent) in 1957. Would the watchdogs of the politically correct allow us to express it that way today? All the more reason for valuing the book as it was written.

Conn's introduction to the country is, typically, New York. For one who lived in gentlemanly splendor on his estate, Rabbit Hill, in Westport, a Connecticut suburb of New York City, the author, or at least his story, takes a dim view of that great American metropolis. Conn's New York is a sinkhole of stinking sewers "with all them buildings shutting you in like a meadow mouse in a maze of soap boxes." (p. 13)

So much for the fabled skyline, the immigrants' first view of their futures. It gets worse. To do business in New York, Conn's uncle Michael has to grease the palms of local politicians, "the kind you'd have to be counting the silver every time they come to dinner." (p. 151)

This exactly catches the spirit of the era, when New York and Chicago duked it out for the prize of being the world's fairest city. New York was thunderstruck that any other city thought itself worthy of the honor, let alone Chicago, a place unknown. Moreover, Chicago burst with a civic pride hard for New York to grasp or match. The best that New York journalists could do was label Chicago "the Windy City," and they didn't mean weather.

Conn shrugs off New York to go and help build the great wheel, fulfilling his prophecy and in pursuit of a German girl he's met in steerage on the Atlantic crossing. Mystery revealed enlivens the end of the story when we realize why Conn had never quite caught Trudy's family name, however enamored he was of her.

Robert Lawson's black-and-white illustrations further enliven the tale, though the young ladies' skirt tails are scandalously short for the 1890s. Mr. Lawson takes another small liberty. Conn dreams of one of the Ferris wheel cars as a honeymoon cottage for Trudy and himself. No idle dream in the end when they receive a car as a gift from its creator.

The story strongly implies that the happy couple received the Ferris Wheel car soon after the fair ended. But in fact, they'd have had to wait another eleven years because the great wheel was reassembled for another fair, the Louisiana Purchase Exposition of 1904, in St. Louis, Missouri. But let's hope their honeymoon lasted at least that long.

In 1941 Robert Lawson's *They Were Strong and Good* won the Caldecott Medal for illustration. In 1945 his *Rabbit Hill* won the Newbery Medal. He remains the only artist-author to receive both the Caldecott Medal and the Newbery Medal. In 2004 the Caldecott winner was Mordecai Gerstein for the illustrations in his *The Man Who Walked Between the Towers,* a haunting account of how Philippe Petit, the aerialist, once danced across a tightrope between the twin towers of the now vanished World Trade Center.

The books keep coming for the young of an America still reaching for the sky.

—Richard Peck

1

He was christened Cornelius—Cornelius Terence Kilroy—but to most he was known as Conn. Only Father Riley ever called him Cornelius. His mother called him Connie, Aunt Honora called him Neil, and Grandfather Giblin seldom called him anything. In fact, Grandfather seldom really spoke at all; he just mumbled and grumbled at the smoldering peat fire and sucked at his clay pipe, which sometimes was lit, but usually was not.

When Conn was twelve years old, Aunt Honora read his fortune from the tea leaves in his cup. She was very old, even then, and the village considered her a Wise Woman.

"Neil, lad," she said, peering into the cup, "mind well what I'm telling you now. Your fortune lies to the west. Keep your face to the sunset and follow the evening star, and one day you'll ride the greatest wheel in all the world."

His mother paused in her knitting. "Not my Connie, Honora," she said worriedly. "Not him, too. West lies America, and must America forever be taking all our fine young men? My brothers Patrick and Michael, your son Dennis and him gone to California and likely skelped by the heathen red Indian savages, the way you've not had a letter from him for a year come Christmas. What's to become of poor Ireland and the Kilroys with all their men gone to America? Sure America's worse than the wars or the Black Famine the way it devours our men—"

"Whisht now," Aunt Honora said placidly, "and don't be talking down the fair young land. Your brothers' fortunes lay to the west like I read in the leaves and they've been great good fortunes. Haven't they prospered and flourished, what with Michael living in an elegant flat house in New York with six daughters and a bathroom? Haven't they sent you the grand presents and money, the way you've been able to buy the red cow and erect a handsome stone for your man, God rest him, in the churchyard at Ballykneedon?"

But Conn's mother refused to be comforted.

"I'd liefer have them back than a herd of stamping red cows and all the presents of Babylon or India," she cried. "And what's this blether about my Connie riding a great wheel? Is it a circus man you'd make of him, or a strolling player performing like a monkey at village fairs on a bicycle or something?''

''I can only read what's in the leaves,'' Aunt Honora answered. ''Take it or leave it, or like it or not, it's what will be.''

''And why wouldn't he go to America?'' piped up Grandfather from the chimney corner. ''Would you have him spending the days of his life cutting peat in old Gallagher's bog when he could be walking the shiny streets of America wearing shoes every day and maybe with a bathroom of his own? If I were a bit younger, I'd be boarding a ship this minute, I would, with a bundle on my shoulder and high hopes in the heart of me.''

Being only twelve at the time, Conn did not worry his head much about Aunt Honora's prophecy. A lusty young lad then, frisky as a colt and the equal of any of the village young ones at running, leaping, or putting the stone, but not much given to thinking.

As the years went by, though, he more and more frequently paused of an evening and gazed into the west over beyond Kilda Point where the sun was dropping into the purple sea. And as the sky faded from gold to green and finally to dusky blue, and the great evening star suddenly began to wink and beckon, the words of his old aunt would recur to him. *Your fortune lies to the west, lad. Keep your face to the sunset and follow the evening star.*

Well, maybe he would and maybe he wouldn't. America and his fortune were calling across the darkening waters, but the call was only a faint one as yet. And what that wheel part was all about he had no notion at all. The biggest wheel he had ever seen was on Mr. Gallagher's peat cart, and that barely breast-high.

Conn was almost eighteen when Father Riley brought the letter. It had been given him by Shamus, the Post, both to save himself a few steps and because Father Riley would have to read it to the family anyway. The arrival of a letter, especially from America, was an event in the village. The Kilroy family crowded the small room; Mother all aflutter, Grandfather in the chimney corner cackling and scolding, Aunt Honora hastily summoned from her home next door. Conn leaned by the open door, the younger children—Willie, Stella, Danny, Agnes, Martin, and Kathleen—sat where they could. A few of the neighbors squeezed in the doorway.

Father Riley hitched his stool closer to the small window, put on his glasses, admonished the squirming children with a stern glance, and opened the letter.

" 'Tis for you, Mary Kate," he said, "I have read it

and it contains no bad news whatsoever, God be praised. 'Tis from your brother Michael in New York. I will read it now:

"My dear Mary Kate,

"I take pen in hand to inform you that we are all well and flourishing, the Saints be praised. The good wife and all six girls are in the best of health, barring a few cases of measles, chicken-pox, croup, colds, rheumatism, and the mumps. My business grows and progresses in a wonderful manner. In recent years I have built more sewers than are in the whole of Ireland, bless the dear country, to say nothing of drains, culverts, curbing, and sidewalks without number.

"The city of New York is a great and growing place and the Michael Giblin Contracting Company Incorporated is growing just as fast. I employ almost three hundred now, all good Mayo men, with a scattering from Roscommon and Clare.

"But I am sore vexed in my mind for lack of a partner to assist me. The burden of managing all this is becoming too heavy for my shoulders alone. Our brother Patrick is the one should be at my side, but he is not of a mind for it. As you know he is a roamer born, not one to settle down to a steady business. Not that I would disparage our own, for he has grown a fine handsome man, with the voice of old Gallagher's bull and a great mattress of a red beard would do a General proud.

"A fine, upstanding man, our James, but bewitched. Bewitched by a madman of an engineer the way he follows him from here to yonder building tunnels and bridges in wild far-off places like Pittsburgh and Kansas City and Kentucky.

"So, dear sister, I am turning to you in my perplexity. Your Cornelius should be near grown a man by now and with the blood of the Kilroys and Giblins both in his veins should be a smart one. Let you send him to me, Mary Kate, to take the place, for a while, of the son I've never had. 'Tis a chance would come to few, but America is the Land of Opportunity and what opportunity has a lad digging peat for old Gallagher his life long, but a bent back and the rheumatics for his old age? A year or so of learning the trade and I pledge you your lad'll never set hand to pick or shovel again but be wearing polished boots and a derby hat, riding his own buggy and overseeing great works. And who knows but one day the firm may be boasting the proud name of Giblin and Kilroy, Inc.?

"I have sent a draft for five hundred dollars to Martin Sheridan the banker man in Galway. Father Riley can draw on it to buy the lad's passage and a suit of new clothing. The rest is for you and your brood with a bit for a few masses for your good man, may he rest in peace.

"I know the thought will wrench your heart, Mary Kate, but you must be thinking of the lad's future and of my crying need.

RL

"May God and His angels keep you and yours is the dearest wish of your loving brother,

Michael James Giblin."

As Father Riley finished, the room rocked with a great uproar, Mother weeping protests, Aunt Honora acclaiming the fulfillment of her prophecy, Grandfather Giblin, who had heard none of it, screeching questions. The children screamed, the neighbors shouted the news all down the street.

Conn, whom it really concerned the most, quietly slipped out and made his way to his favorite seat on the stone wall overlooking the bay. The setting sun set his coppery hair all aglow and washed his blue eyes to a pale seagreen. His fortune was calling loudly now, the shimmering golden road to the west spread before him. His heart leaped with the thrill of great changes to come. He became aware of a kindly hand on his shoulder.

" 'Tis all settled, lad," the priest said. "We will leave with the dawning. Partings are best done with quickly."

2

As the good ship *City of Bristol* listed to the first ocean swell, Conn leaned on the rail and took his last look at the lovely green fields of Ireland. For a moment a great wave of homesickness swept him. He was not alone in this; along the crowded rail there sounded many a hastily caught sob. Mothers and children wept unashamed.

A small wizened crooked man next to him pulled down his cap, lit his pipe, and glanced at Conn with a keen but friendly eye. "A pretty sight yon," he said, "coming or going. But better from a real ship under sail. You've no time then to be getting sentimental. 'Tis the first time, this, that I've behelt it and me a passenger. The first time too from the deck of one of these belching, stenching tea kettles, them with a shaking vibration would loosen the teeth of a bronze statue. *Steamships!*" he snorted disgustedly. He slapped a few cinders from his coat sleeve and started forward, walking with a queer, one-sided, crablike gait.

Could it possibly be only yesterday that the letter had come? Only this morning that he and Father Riley had left the village in the misty dawn?

His mother, of course, had wept; the children, those who were awake, had joined in without quite knowing why; Grandfather Giblin had screeched admonitions. Aunt Honora, wrapped in a blanket, had called from her window to remember her prophecy. As he and Father Riley stepped briskly down the highway old Gallagher's bog was still in shadow. The dim forms of the peat cutters starting their work called good wishes.

It was a glorious May morning, the sun warm on their backs, the fields dazzling in their greenness. Conn, as they left the village behind, threw back his head and sang for the sheer joy of living. Father Riley, when there were no passers-by, joined in with his deep, sonorous voice. "In the eyes of some it might not be seemly," he chuckled, "but God's birds are singing their throats hoarse and who are we, the least worthy of his creatures, to be shaming them with a gloomy silence?"

In Galway, Conn, dazed by the crowds, the thunder of

drays, and the shouting of the teamsters, was only dimly aware that Uncle Michael's draft had been cashed, his passage purchased and he himself completely outfitted in new clothing, boots, and linen, all of good quality, modest of cut, and blastedly uncomfortable. A small carpetbag held a few extras, and Father Riley's worn wallet still contained a heartening sum for Mother and the young ones.

Then suddenly they were on the pier in the midst of a surging, weeping, laughing, calling mob of emigrants, their relatives, and well-wishers. They paused a moment in a slight eddy in the lee of a bollard.

"My son," said Father Riley, "I have taught you your letters and a bit of figuring. I wish I could have done more. I have taught you the rudiments of civilized behavior and to honor God and your elders. Now remember this: Ireland may be a poor country, but she exports a crop second to none on earth—her men and women. Never shame her. Take pride in the blood in your veins and the land of your birth. Now get you aboard and God go with you."

As the gray buildings of Galway shrank in the distance and the crowd on the pier became a formless dark mass, Conn could still make out the tall black figure of the good priest, his hand raised in benediction.

Conn sat on a hatch as the *City of Bristol* plodded steadily through the night. He could not quite face the packed airless steerage, the hard three-tiered bunks, the smell, the weeping, the seasickness that had already begun although the sea was as calm as the pools in Gallagher's bog.

The crooked little man was seated close by, sucking on his unlit pipe. He fished a short length of light line from his pocket and idly began tying knots, the most complicated, elaborate knots Conn had ever seen. He did not look at his work, his eyes wandered about the deck, to the moon-bright horizon, to the dimly lit pilot house, but his hands flashed as rapidly and surely as Aunt Honora's at her weaving.

"Would you be a sailor man, mister?" Conn asked finally.

The other smiled and lighted his pipe. "I was," he said, "till a fall gave me this one-sided, crabwise carcass. Then no Master would sign me on. 'A.B.?' they'd say. 'Able-bodied seaman, you? Sorry, no.' Though I could make it to the masthead as quick as the next, and reef, hand, and steer with the best of them.

"So I took me a shore job in the yards at Belfast. A rigger—master rigger now. Many's the fine ship we turned out there, big grain clippers mostly, for the Australian grain trade. Steel-hulled, standing rigging all steel cable—nasty stuff to handle, but strong."

"Are you for New York?" asked Conn.

"Aye," said the little man. "Just for the change. Often enough I've called there, but never to stay. I'll have work—there's still plenty of real ships to be rigged. They're not all these floating jam factories, yet. What of you—New York too?"

"Yes, for the now," Conn answered, "but I don't know—"

It was good to have someone to talk to, for Conn was lonesome in spite of the packed steerage. He was beginning to learn that there's nothing so lonesome as a crowd. He talked of his life at home, of mother and Grandfather Giblin and Father Riley and the peat-cutting in old Gallagher's bog. He told the little man of Uncle Michael's letter and Uncle Michael's plans for him, and of Aunt Honora's prophecy.

" 'Tis a grand fortune your aunt has read you," the little man said, "but it must go beyont New York, surely, and building sewers. 'Twould be hard to be keeping your face to the sunset and you in a sewer trench, or to follow the evening star with all them buildings shutting you in like a meadow mouse in a maze of soap boxes."

"And what would you make of the big wheel part?" Conn asked.

"That is a puzzler surely," the other admitted. "It could be maybe the wheel of fortune—on top today and at the bottom tomorrow, that's the way of things in America—but I don't know—"

They soon became good friends, Conn and the crooked little man; Martin Brennan was his name. They both preferred the small open deck-space allotted the steerage passengers to the stifling quarters below and spent most of their time seated on the hatch, regardless of weather. Martin tried to teach Conn to tie knots, bends, and hitches, but they were so many and so elaborate that it seemed well-nigh hopeless. He did succeed though in mastering a few that he hoped would be useful in construction work.

"With all of them that I know," Martin said with a grin, "there's one that's always eluded me, and that's the one the priest ties. A good thing though, for what fine girl would want to be hitched to a slue-sided thing the like of me?"

The steerage was a jumble of races—mostly Irish and Scandinavians, a few Poles and Slavs, and some Germans. "Many a good crew I've sailed with of that same mixture," Martin Brennan laughed. "Micks, Squareheads, Polacks, and Dutchmen. A year or two now and they'll all be good Americans. A wonderful country is

America, like a great stew pot, the way you can be throwing in all them elements and it turning out a fine healthy dish. Barring a bit of scum, of course, that has to be whisked off."

Conn was idly scanning the crowd when all at once his eyes lit on the girl. How blonde she is, was his first thought, and How scrubbed she is, was his second. She was both. Great heavy braids of pale flaxen hair ringed her head, her skin was the palest of pinks, her eyes the clear blue of moor ponds on a winter day. Her quaint peasant clothes were almost aggressive in their starched and laundered cleanliness.

Fittingly enough she was carrying a bucket of water, a large cake of soap, and a clean towel. She was followed by a small towheaded boy of three or so, whom she led to the rail, stripped of jacket and shirt, and scrubbed vigorously. She rubbed him to a fine pink polish with the towel, then sent him skipping below.

"Ach, this sea water," she exclaimed, as she emptied the bucket into the scuppers, "for washing it is not goot."

"For fish to swim in and for ships to sail on," Martin said with a grin, "sea water can't be beat. It is also handy for separating the continents of the world one from the other. Otherwise it's of no use at all. And how is it a young German girl the like of you is speaking English so good?"

She smiled pleasantly at the little man but her eyes were mostly for Conn. "A long time we plan to come to America. So I study English in the schule. It is very bad, no?"

"Good as the Queen's," Conn answered. "And is it New York where you're staying?"

"No. We go to Witsconsin. My Oncle Otto is there. You know Witsconsin?"

" 'Tis no seaport," Martin said, scratching his head. "To the west I'm thinking, out in the middle of the country somewhere."

"By Chickago, I think," the girl said. "My Oncle Otto has cows—many cows. We will make cheeses. My father is a fine cheese-maker. I will milk the cows. Are Indians in Witsconsin?"

"I don't know," Conn answered, "this is my first trip."

She disappeared below but emerged shortly, her bucket filled with clothes which she proceeded to scrub and hang on the rail to dry.

"If there *is* Indians in Wisconsin," Martin mused, "they'd best be moving along or she'll be trying to scrub the red off them—once she's finished bathing the cows. A pretty lass though, in spite of her obsession for soap."

"She is so," Conn agreed. "The like of a wee chiny

figure I was seeing once in a shop window in Ballykneedon. The same pink cheeks on her and blue eyes the size of doorknobs. I wish she was for New York."

"Well, Wisconsin is to the west." Martin chuckled. "And what was it your aunt's fortune was saying? *Keep your face to the sunset and follow the evening star*—and you'll come to Wisconsin—and get your ears washed."

After that Conn saw a good deal of her. He met her father and mother, stout, kindly souls who radiated good will. He met her five younger brothers and sisters, a tow-headed flight of steps of from three to thirteen years whose only English consisted of "goot morning" and "thank you."

Often, when she was not scrubbing the younger ones or after they had been put to bed below, she joined him on the hatch or at the rail. He had never talked much with girls before, and now, to his surprise, found it quite easy and most enjoyable. Her name, he learned, was Trudy. She was sixteen. They came from the Black Forest. Her father abhorred war, armies, violence of any sort. Grandfather had been killed in France in 1870.

"So—we come to America," she smiled. "In America one is free, no?" Little Franz, Karl, and Heinrich would never be conscripted: Father would not have to leave his cattle and crops every summer to go on the maneuvers that he hated.

Conn, on his side, told her of his life in the village, of his mother and Aunt Honora and Grandfather Giblin and of the young ones. He talked of the peat-cutting and of fishing at night for the great river salmon when one had to outwit not only the fish but the gamekeepers as well. An easy, carefree life in a beautiful land, but always, just around the corner, the hunger. "It is a hard thing," he said, "to hear the young ones crying for the want of food and to be digging the potatoes and them all black and shriveled and slimy with the blight."

"Jah, jah," she said quickly. "I know. We have had the hunger too. But in America will be plenty, no? Oncle Otto says so."

On the last evening out she joined him at the rail as the ship plowed down the golden pathway that led to the setting sun. It was then that he told her of Aunt Honora's prophecy.

"It is a beautiful fortune," she said. "*Your fortune lies to the west.* Witsconsin lies to the west too. You will come to Witsconsin some day, no?"

"I might," he laughed. "And be finding you married to a fine fat Dutchman, with six young ones of your own to wash and a whole herd of cows to be milking."

"*Nein*—no," she said solemnly. "I will wait and you will follow the evening star, and you will come—it is your fortune."

"And where would I be finding you?" he asked.

"Oh, in Witsconsin," she answered. "Just ask anyone for my Oncle Otto."

3

Conn stood at his bedroom window watching the sun go down over the Palisades. Uncle Michael's flat was high up, on the fifth floor, so that the one window of the rear bedroom allowed a western view all the way over to New Jersey. The smoking chimneys of the lower brownstone fronts stretching down the block were sharply silhouetted against the cold December sky. The streets were now engulfed in shadow; at Ninth Avenue a brightly lighted Elevated train rattled by, its busy little engine coughing clouds of blue steam and scattering a trail of bright sparks.

He made his way to the bathroom to wash up for dinner. It was a great convenience surely, the bathroom, with its marble-topped basin and its shiny zinc tub set solidly in varnished matchboarding. As he turned up the

Welsbach light and listened to its slight pop, he smiled to think how impressed he had been, on his first arrival, by all this grandeur which he now took for granted.

He certainly had been a greenhorn in those days, only seven months ago to be sure, but at eighteen one can cover a lot of ground in seven months. It seemed like seven years in some ways.

He still remembered Uncle Michael's loud and hearty greeting at the pier, the more restrained but cordial welcomes of his cousins Stella and Agnes. Agnes, pretty, impish, and a bit younger than he, was hard put to it to hide her amusement at his appearance. The heavy tweeds and boots from Galway's leading emporium were hardly of New York's latest mode. The curly copper-colored hair which Aunt Honora had cut only a month or so ago ran somewhat wild over his collar. The almost empty carpetbag stamped him as an immigrant fresh from the old sod.

He was quite bewildered by the noisy bustle and confusion which made Galway's waterfront seem like a sleepy fishing village in comparison. The tinkling bells of the horsecars and the clanging rush of the new cable cars contended with the eager shouts of the cabmen, porters, and hotel runners. Great drays rumbled and jarred on the granite block pavements; newsboys and bootblacks shrilled and fought.

Uncle Michael shepherded Conn and his cousins through the throng to a waiting fringe-topped surrey. It was driven by a heavily mustached, derby-hatted individual, obviously a Giblin Company foreman. Uncle Michael climbed up beside him, and Conn sat in the back seat between the girls. "A rose between two thorns," Agnes giggled.

"Over to the Avenue, Jim," Uncle Michael ordered, "so the lad can see a bit of the city."

As they swung into the stream of traffic on Fifth Avenue the girls primped a bit and sat up straighter. Uncle Michael lighted a cigar, gave one to Jim, and assumed the role of guide, pointing out the various stores and hotels, the churches, and the palatial homes of the well-to-do. Many of these explanations ended with the proud phrase, "Pavements, curbing, and drains by the Giblin Contracting Company Incorporated."

"We are now approaching the residence of Mr. William K. Vanderbilt," he would announce with a wave of the cigar. "Excavation, drains, paving, and curbing by the Giblin Contracting Company." Or, "West Thirty-fourth Street. One thousand five hundred and forty eight yards of six-foot, brick-arch sewer by Giblin Contracting Company."

Occasionally his discourse might be varied by a disparaging bit, such as, "West Forty-first Street. Eight hundred yards of miserable, slatternly-laid thirty-inch tile by Regan and Schaumholtz. A disgrace to the city the way it clogs and backs up after every moderate heavy dew!"

Conn was filled with awe by the great busy stores, the marble and granite châteaux and palaces, the never-ending stream of glittering carriages with their high-stepping horses. But the awe almost mounted to panic when they finally drew up before the apartment house where the Giblins resided. Seven impressive stories it towered, all of brick and brownstone, its façade tastefully decorated with wrought-iron fire escapes. A uniformed doorman helped the young ladies dismount and carried Conn's bag in to the elevator.

An elevator! Conn paled a bit and crossed himself surreptitiously, but Uncle Michael and the girls entered the open-grilled cage unconcernedly and he needs must follow. The operator slid the door closed, heaved on the great rope, and the cage wobbled its way safely to the fifth floor, where Aunt Cecilia greeted him warmly.

She was simple and easygoing, like Mother and Aunt Honora and the other village women. Wealth had not spoiled her, but it did have its drawbacks, for with a cook and housemaid to do everything, poor Aunt Cecilia found it hard to keep herself occupied and was putting on weight much too rapidly.

The Giblin flat (apartment, Agnes called it) was large

and rather floridly furnished. With the four younger girls away at the convent it seemed almost overlarge. To Conn, after the two-roomed cottage, it was immense.

Uncle Michael showed him his room—a small one at the back of the apartment—proudly initiated him in the mysteries of the bathroom, and cautioned him on the dangers of gas lighting: "Never turn the flame too low if there's a draft, careful of the lace curtains, if you smell gas open the window but never strike a match," and so forth.

Conn learned to manipulate the gas and the plumbing quickly and easily. In fact, he learned everything from table manners to the ways of New York traffic quickly and easily. Uncle Michael had been right when he surmised that the blood of the Kilroys and the Giblins would produce a smart young man. But even he was astonished to discover how rapidly his nephew could grasp the details of his contracting business.

Within a few short months Conn had familiarized himself with all the forms and uses of brick, tile pipe, stonemasonry, and concrete that went into the building of sewers, drains, and paving. He was equally at home with the Mayo men in a deep shored-up ditch or with the engineers and draftsmen in the office. His glowing copper hair (roached now in the latest New York fashion), his broad freckled grin, and his eager youthful friendliness won him friends everywhere.

Uncle Michael was delighted. "An alderman in ten years, I'm betting, at the rate he's going," he confided to Aunt Cecilia, "and a partner in the Giblin Company in five. A real Shylock too, when it comes to driving a bargain. Only today he wheedled a bargeload of brick out of one of them up-river Dutchmen for ten per cent less than I could have got it. And what's more he made 'em like it."

More and more Uncle Michael grew to depend on his nephew. Conn now had a horse and buggy of his own to visit the various jobs and to drive in Central Park or about town of a Sunday.

Often these Sunday rides took him over to the East River shipyard where Martin Brennan worked. Martin was too much in love with his work to leave it for long, even of a Sunday. Seated on a box in the warm sun, gazing up at the towering masts of some great ship undergoing repair, he would point out and explain to Conn the beauty and efficiency of its elaborate network of rigging. And Conn, being a smart young man, soon began to grasp the functions of all the myriad spars, shrouds, stays, braces, blocks, tackle, chains, rods, eyebolts, turnbuckles, and the hundred other things that went into the rigging of a ship.

Or Martin might wave to the newly finished Brooklyn Bridge, whose huge towers dominated the whole skyline. "One of the wonders of the world," he would declaim, "and rightly so indeed. A masterpiece of rigging that, beautiful as any ship." He pointed out to Conn how each graceful cable supported its true share of the tremendous weight, how each was proportioned to do its own task exactly, not a strand or a pound too much or too little.

Many times they walked the broad promenade to Brooklyn and back while Martin explained the function of each cable, suspender, bridle, and girder. He showed how the great supporting cables ran over huge iron saddles at the tower tops, free to slide slightly as the long structure swelled or shrank from broiling sun or icy blast.

" 'Twere not for that," he exclaimed, "they'd have them towers tore down like the walls of Jericho in a month's time. As it is she's strong as a mountain range. Strong but soople. Soopleness does it, the way she'll be standing handsome and useful when we're in our graves and our children and their children after them."

Occasionally, too, they would take a walk along First Avenue or the Bowery to watch the throng of Sunday strollers and the passing stream of carriages and cyclists. The new low-wheeled "safeties" were all the rage now, but a few elderly conservatives still stuck to the old-fashioned high-wheeled bicycle.

"There you are, Conn, me lad," laughed Martin, waving at an unusually tall one. "I'm surprised you've not acquired one of them contraptions and you the dude you're getting to be. It would make your aunt's prophecy come true, surely, for there's no bigger wheel in all the world, that is, for the purpose of riding."

"Thanks, no." Conn grinned. "There's easier ways of breaking your neck than taking a header off one of them."

Martin's shrewd little eyes settled on Conn closely. "And what about that grand fortune your aunt read you?" he asked. "Do you think you've gone far enough to the west now? Sure you're doing well here and you with a wealthy uncle fair panting for you to become his partner, with a fine job and two pretty and adoring cousins hanging on your every word and glance. Or have you still got your mind tied to the evening star?"

"I don't know—I don't know at all," Conn answered slowly, his forehead all puckered with thinking. "I've got everything here anyone ought to want, I guess. More than I deserve, likely. But—somehow—I don't know. What with the crowds and the noise and the dirt and the hurry and all—it's hard to think.

"But Martin—I don't want to be spending all the days of my life building sewers and laying pavements, it's little more exciting than cutting peat in old Gallagher's bog, and not as pleasant. There anyway you could breathe the air and sometimes see and hear a wee bird and him singing, or perhaps a rabbit poking his head at you through a hedge. And you could watch the sun sinking into the decent clean ocean and not being smothered in a cloud of dirty chimney smoke.''

Martin Brennan chuckled understandingly. ''Not that I hold anything against sewers and pavements, mind you,'' he said. ''They have their uses, but for you to be building them doesn't seem becoming to the grandness of your aunt's prophecy. 'Go west, young man,' as Horace Greeley was saying—or was it Henry Ward Beecher? 'Go west and grow up with the country.'

''Follow your fortune, lad, there's greater things to be done than laying sidewalks for mean little people to be scuffing their dirty boots on. Was there the likes of a respectable shipyard to the west of here I'd be follying the evening star meself.''

It was that very evening, halfway through Sunday night supper, that Uncle Patrick came roaring in out of the west.

4

Uncle Patrick was big. Everything about him was big; jutting beak of a nose, high arched chest, huge, corded, powerful hands. He'd a neck like a sea lion and a voice that carried like the fog siren on Kilda Point. His square-cut red beard was thick as a mattress, his laugh rattled the supper dishes, but his tread, strange enough, was light and sure as a cat's.

He embraced Aunt Cecilia, then Stella and Agnes, swinging them clear off the floor, shook his brother by the shoulders, and then turned to greet Conn.

"So this is Mary Kate's boy," he shouted. "Cornelius Terence Kilroy. He has the Giblin hair and eyes indeed, but the small size of him must be Kilroy. And the white color. Mike, have you been keeping him buried in one of your manholes the way he has the pallor of a bleached oyster on him?"

"He's been doing a bit of office work lately," Uncle Michael said, "and very well too."

"Office work?" Patrick snorted. "Offices are for sniveling clerks and mice and cobwebs. Show me your hands, lad."

Conn held out his hands, palms up, feeling a little ashamed of their white softness. All the traces of peat-cutting had long since disappeared. Only last week he had been rather pleased when Agnes had commented favorably on their genteel appearance—and now he was ashamed.

"Humph!" Uncle Patrick snorted. "The hands of a pianny player. You wouldn't have been doing a bit of embroidery now, would you?"

"I can handle a slane with the best," Conn answered, coloring. "My palms may be a bit soft at the moment, but my knuckles are hard enough."

Uncle Patrick gave a great roar of laughter and clapped him on the shoulder. "All right, my little fighting cock," he cried, "there speaks the Giblin blood, but we'll not be proving it now."

Uncle Michael poured himself another cup of tea and motioned Aunt Cecilia and the girls to leave. "Now Patrick," he said, "don't be upsetting the lad and filling his head with notions. He's doing well here where he is, very well, I'm proud of him. He's a wonderful fine opportunity with me in a well-established business. He's no call to be blistering his hands with pick or shovel or roaming the wild country leaping from one job to the other—"

"Opportunity is it?" Uncle Patrick roared. "Opportunity! Is it opportunity you call it to be making a pasty office clerk of him, poring in ledgers and dickering over the price of a barrow-load of bricks? Or scratching ditches in your dirty city streets like a lap dog trying to bury a bone, when there's men's work crying to be done?"

Uncle Michael answered heatedly, "There's as much glory in a well-built sewer, Pat Giblin, as any of your grand tunnels or bridges. I'll not have the lad snatched away from us to go following your harebrained engineer, whatever his name is, from hither to yon."

"For your information," Uncle Patrick shouted, "the name is Ferris, George Washington Gale Ferris. Also for your information, he's the most brilliant young engineer walking the earth today, the way he'd make your Thomas A. Edisons and your Alexander Graham Bells look like petty tinkerers. Only twelve years out of college and he has as great a knowledge of the ways of iron and steel as the god Vulcan himself. He can throw a steel bridge across a raging river as easy as you could knock together a plank walk across one of your two-penny sewer trenches—yes, and be planning out a tunnel or a railroad line in his head while doing it. 'Tis a wonderful thing to be associating with such a genius, and it's the proudest honor ever happened to a Giblin to be called his good right hand, which is the way he mentions me.

"Moreover," went on Uncle Patrick, pacing the floor, "when his present project is completed it will be the century's greatest wonder and his name will be on the lips of the world from here to Timbuctoo."

"Will it so?" Uncle Michael said sarcastically. "And what is this monstrous world's wonder, if I may ask?"

"You may ask and not learn," his brother answered. "I'm not free to tell at the moment."

"And what is the good right hand of this great genius doing in New York? How can the poor man manage to lace his boots without you and him in the wilds of the west somewhere?"

"I'm in New York on business for him," said Uncle Patrick. "Chiefly to pick up a few good men—riggers, if I can find them. Real men with the heart to do their work at dizzying heights and eat their lunches sitting on a girder no bigger than your two hands with nothing below them but the empty air and maybe a stray sea gull or two. I'd hopes that the lad here might crave a job with a bit of adventure to it, but I'm feared he hasn't the heart."

"He has the sense—" Uncle Michael began, but Conn

pushed past him and faced the red-bearded giant. His face was pale now, his fists tightly clenched.

"I have the heart for any job any man can do, Uncle Patrick," he said quietly. "And if I hadn't promised Father Riley to honor my elders I'd tell it you in stronger words. What's more I've sat at dizzy heights and smoked a pipe with my friend Martin Brennan the rigger on the crosstrees of many a tall-masted ship, and thought no more of it than I'd be sitting on a bench in Central Park feeding the squirrels."

Uncle Patrick clapped his nephew on the shoulders with mighty hands. "I thought I'd strike a spark of the old Giblin in you," he laughed. "But what's this about a friend is a rigger? That's what I'm looking for. Does he know his work? Where can I find him?"

"He's the best, I understand," Conn answered. "Five years master rigger in the Belfast yards. A wee little man, crooked from a fall, but quick as a monkey and hands on him can handle steel cable like an old lady with her knitting.

"But you'd be wasting your time," he added. "He's choosy as to who he works for."

"Now laddie," Uncle Patrick chuckled, "I'm no ogre. You'll find I bark worse than I bite. Where at does the little man work?"

"Webb's shipyard, on the East River," Conn said.

"But don't be telling him I sent you. We're good friends and I'd not have him thinking ill of me."

"He'll thank you from the bottom of his heart," Uncle Patrick laughed, "when he hears what I'm offering him. I'll have him tomorrow. And now—what about you? Are you of a mind to go west with us to a real job with glory to it, or are you for becoming a soft-handed office clerk and seeing the world from a drainage ditch?"

"I'm beholden to Uncle Michael for fetching me here across the sea," Conn answered. "And for treating me like a son of his own—and to Aunt Cecilia and the girls for being mother and sisters to me. But—"

"You're beholden to no one," Uncle Michael interrupted sadly. "You've earned back your passage many times. Any little things we've done for you are out of our love for you as a son, but like any son you've got a right to a free choice. You're young and your heart's crying for adventures and I'd not be standing in your way however you choose."

"When I was a lad of twelve," Conn said slowly, "Aunt Honora read my fortune in the tea leaves and this was the way of it, '*Your fortune lies to the west, lad,*' she said. '*Keep your face to the sunset and follow the evening star and one day you'll ride the greatest wheel in all the world.*' "

Uncle Patrick stood thunderstruck. His chin dropped,

he stared at Conn with wondering eyes. "What is that you're saying?" he finally asked, "—that last part?"

"Follow the evening star," Conn repeated, *"and one day you'll ride the greatest wheel in all the world."*

"It is a miracle surely," Uncle Patrick said in an awed voice. "A wonder indeed. Six years ago and her on the other side of the world, to be foretelling the future as clear as any soothsayer of the olden days or the prophets of Holy Writ."

"An old woman's notion that makes no sense," Uncle Michael said. "Where is the wonder in it?"

"I shouldn't tell you, but I must," Uncle Patrick answered solemnly, "and I'll trust you to keep it to yourself for the now. The wonder in it is this. Follow the evening star, and you come to Chicago. And in Chicago, at this moment, my boss, Mr. George Washington Gale Ferris, is setting out to build the greatest wheel in all the world!"

5

Dinner the next night was a dreary affair. Uncle Michael, Aunt Cecilia, and the girls spoke in toneless voices. Agnes's eyes were suspiciously pink. Uncle Patrick, though, was in a high good humor.

"Your crooked little man is a jewel, Conn," he cried. "Knows his work up and down and has the confidence of an elephant, which is what he'll have the need of, on this job. 'Give me something to hang it on,' the wee fellow said, 'and I'll rig you a tackle would lift the earth off its axis.' He'll be bringing three of his men as well, so it's a grand find I've made and all due to you, my lad. We're grateful to you, Mr. Ferris and I are."

Conn was wearing his heavy Galway clothes. His carpetbag held some well-worn work shirts, sweaters, and overalls. All his fashionable New York clothes were packed in a trunk which Aunt Cecilia promised to look after.

He had spent the day at the office going over things with a disconsolate Uncle Michael. "Young Tommy Glynn can take my place fine, Uncle Michael," he had said. "He knows the work as well as I do and he's a harder driver, he'll get more done for you."

"We'll make out, I suppose," Uncle Michael answered with a sigh, "but he's not of our blood, and an Ulsterman to boot. I had hoped for one of our own at my shoulder, but if it's not to be it's not to be. Only I wish to God Honora had broke her blasted teacup before she went to reading your fate in the leaves."

Now, over the dessert, Uncle Michael turned to his brother. "Patrick," he asked, "just what is this great project, this wheel you spoke of? I understand none of it at all."

Uncle Patrick smiled. "I can tell you no more of it for the now," he said. "I shouldn't have mentioned it at all, only that Honora's prophecy shocked it out of me. Once Mr. Ferris has announced it official it will fill all the newspapers and you can read about it and talk about it to your heart's content. Talk about it you surely will, along with all the rest of the world, and I'll warrant your talk will be loud with pride that your crazy brother Pat and your young nephew are in the heart of the building of it."

"Will there be danger in it, Patrick?" Aunt Cecilia asked anxiously.

He avoided a direct reply. "There's a bit of danger in all real work," he admitted. "Conn could easily have had a sewer ditch cave in on him or a paving slab slip and break his two legs, which would have been a mean and unglorious fate for a Kilroy. I'll be keeping an eye on him out there, never fear."

The whole family accompanied them to Grand Central Station for the midnight train. Conn's heart gave a great throb of excitement as they stepped into the cavernous echoing train shed. From high up among the girders, flickering arc lights shed a violet semblance of moonlight. Hissing, panting locomotives coughed towering columns of smoke and steam. A train newly arrived from the west was caked with snow and ice. Conn tightened the muffler that Agnes had knitted for him snugly around his throat. It was bitterly cold.

Halfway down the platform they came on Martin Brennan and his crew seated patiently on their bundles. Two of them were huge, square-headed, blond Norwegians, so alike they might have been twins. The third was a thin-nosed Cockney, missing several teeth and musically in-

RL

clined. At the moment he was singing "A Bicycle Built for Two," very badly.

Martin Brennan rose as they approached and greeted Uncle Patrick with a grin. "All present and accounted for, Mr. Giblin," he announced. "Scrymer here a trifle overcome with emotion—and porter—but put your mind at rest, he never indulges on the job."

"See to that," Uncle Patrick said. "Once we reach Chicago he'll drink nothing but the salubrious waters of Lake Michigan. Now get them aboard." The two stolid Norwegians gathered up their bundles—and Mr. Scrymer, who was now embarked on "Rule, Britannia"—and mounted the steps of the smoker.

There were affectionate farewells all around, tearful ones on the part of Aunt Cecilia and the girls. "Patrick," said Uncle Michael ferociously, "mind Mary Kate's lad well. Does anything befall him I'll have that beard of yours to stuff a horse collar and your thick hide for a pair of traces."

Suddenly they were in the dimly lit car, settling themselves on the hard seats, and the train was moving. Conn hastily wiped a clear spot on the steamy window, caught one glimpse of three waving handkerchiefs, and then they were gone.

He and Martin Brennan sat facing Uncle Patrick, whose huge bulk filled a whole seat. Behind them the two

Norwegians sat in unblinking silence. Scrymer, his head cushioned on their bundles, snored peacefully. Overhead, smoky kerosene lamps shed an uncertain light; at either end of the car the small coal stoves glowed red. The air grew steamy, heavy with tobacco smoke. The wheels clicked steadily, the couplings rattled and clanged.

"Uncle Patrick," Conn asked, "couldn't you be telling us a bit more about Mr. Ferris's great wheel, now that we're working for him and all?"

His Uncle smiled as he lit his pipe. "I could indeed," he said, "and here's the way of it.

"You've doubtless been reading in the newspapers of the colossal World's Columbian Exposition to open in Chicago in the spring, May first, 1893, the greatest world's fair ever was thought of?

"Well the directors and committees and the archytects and millionaires that are running the affair decided they wanted some huge and wonderful attraction would put the Frenchmen and their Eiffel Tower to shame. So they came to the boss, naturally, and they said, 'Mr. Ferris, for our Fair we want to build a stupendous, spectacular feature, totally different from anything was ever done before, only bigger. Can you suggest something?'

" 'I could,' says the boss, and he goes down to West Virginia and builds a couple of bridges while he's thinking it over. Then he comes back to Chicago and has lunch with the director and the committee and the engineers and the archytects and all.

" 'Well Mr. Ferris,' asks the director, 'have you an idea?'

" 'I have,' says the boss. 'Wait till I finish my chops and I'll tell it you.'

"So he finished his chops, hauled out a pencil and a bit of paper, and sketched out a picture of his colossus of a wheel.

" 'It will be a tension wheel two hundred and fifty feet high,' he said. 'That's seven times bigger than any wheel ever was known; taller than any building in Chicago. Was it set in Broadway in New York a man on top of it could reach out his foot and give a kick to the weathervane atop the spire of Trinity Church.

" 'The axle will be set on towers one hundred and forty-three feet high,' the boss goes on, pointing it out with his fork. 'Around the rim of the wheel will be hung thirty-six cars, each one as big as a streetcar and holding thirty-six passengers. Those passengers will have a ride they'll remember all the days of their lives, the way they'll be boasting on it to their children and their grandchildren.'

" 'They will not,' said the director, 'because the thing will never be built.'

" 'It's impossible,' the engineers said.

" 'Preposterous,' shout the archytects.

" 'Absurd,' yelled the committee. 'Nobody'd put up any money for such a harebrained contraption.'

" 'Very good, gentlemen,' says the boss, helping himself to a toothpick, 'I've got other fish to fry. Thanks for the lunch.' And he gets his hat and goes home.

"Well, they argued and bellowed and shilly-shallied, while the time slipped by. They consulted all the biggest engineers in the country and they all said it couldn't be done.

"In the meantime Mr. Ferris sat in his office and drew up all his plans down to the last bolt, nut, and rivet. Then he tucked 'em under his arm and went to see the director and the committee. 'Well, gentlemen,' he said, 'it's now November and your Fair opens May first. What do you say?'

" 'We have consulted the best engineering brains in the country and they all say it can't be done,' said the director.

" 'The best engineering brains in the country are right here,' the boss said, tapping his forehead. 'And they say it can.'

"Well, they couldn't deny that, and they'd raised some of the money, so they gave him a concession. He ordered his steel from six of the best steel mills in the country and they, knowing him well, went at making it hammer and tongs. Then, when everything was going smooth, the committee ran out of money and they got timorous again and took back their concession. But the boss just went ahead and ordered his stone and sand and cement and begun digging the foundations for his towers. Then he put on his hat and goes to see the committee again.

" 'Gentlemen,' he said, 'it's now *December* and your Fair opens May first. Do you want your wheel or don't you?'

" 'We do,' they said, 'but we've got no more money.'

" 'Well, raise it,' he said, 'or your wheel won't be finished till after the ball is over. And give me back my concession by the fifteenth or I'll go about me business.'

"So that's the state things were in when I left last week," concluded Uncle Patrick. "We may get there tomorrow and find we've got no jobs, but I don't think so. When the boss sets his hand to a thing it gets done, somehow."

"Uncle Patrick," Conn asked, "you were after saying that Mr. Ferris's wheel is a tension wheel. What is it you'd call a tension wheel?"

Uncle Patrick scratched his ear with his pipe. "The best I can explain it is this," he said. "You've seen plenty of bicycle wheels and doubtless have been wondering how a wheel like that with wee thin spokes of wire, little thicker than a lady's hatpin, could be holding up the weight of a big full-grown man. Well it's because in a bicycle wheel the weight is *hung* on all those little spokes.

Any one of them would hold the weight of a man or two men even, was it hung on 'em, although they wouldn't support the weight of a pound of tobaccy if stood on end. A bicycle wheel is a tension wheel. With all those wire spokes stretched tight as the wires in a pianny, it'll be as strong as a clumsy wagon wheel but that light you can lift it with your little finger."

"Soople too," put in Martin Brennan, "like I was saying about the Brooklyn Bridge."

"Soople too," agreed Uncle Patrick. "And no more resistance to the wind than a canary cage. Which is of great importance to Mr. Ferris's wheel the way them gales from Lake Michigan would strip the fur off a buffalo."

Uncle Patrick snuggled his chin into his beard and dozed off. From the seat behind, Mr. Scrymer's snores rose steadily. Conn wiped a clear spot on the steamy window and looked out. They had left Albany behind and were now winding westward through the Mohawk valley. The moon was bright; wood lots were etched sharply against the rolling, snow-covered hills. Along the eaves of dark barns rows of icicles glittered. It looked cold.

Conn slept and dreamed of a peat cart with bicycle wheels ten feet high. Old Gallagher was hitched between the shafts instead of the donkey and Martin Brennan was driving. The cart was loaded with Wisconsin cheeses.

6

It was late the next evening when they disembarked in Chicago—theirs had not been a fast train. Stiff, sore, and sleepy, Conn received only a vague impression of the city, for Uncle Patrick herded them onto various clanging streetcars which clattered and banged and bumped a circuitous way to the far outskirts, a region of dimly lit rutted streets, scattered and ramshackle buildings.

Their boarding house was larger and less decrepit than its neighbors; it was wrapped in a steamy aroma of simmering prunes and corned beef and cabbage, but it was moderately clean and blissfully warm. Uncle Patrick was boisterously greeted by the landlady, Mrs. Murphy, by her husband, three dogs, and half a dozen cats.

"Sure it's a happy evening sees you back, Mr. Giblin,"

Mrs. Murphy cried, "though we're woeful cramped for space. Your nephew, now, and the wee man can share your room, if you've no objection, but I'm afraid the others will have to put up with the bunkhouse we've made out of the old stable."

"Plenty good enough for uncouth furriners the like of them," Uncle Patrick roared. "The height of elegance compared to a ship's fo'c'stle or the East River rat holes they're used to." Mr. Murphy fetched a lantern and led Scrymer and the two grinning Norwegians out to the back premises.

" 'Tis not the Palmer House nor yet a grand apartment like your Uncle Michael's," Uncle Patrick yawned as they prepared for bed, "but it's close to the work and it's fortunate we are to have any place at all, the way workmen have gathered here from the four corners of the nation to be working on the Fair buildings and grounds. Come spring and the visitors begin arriving, Mrs. Murphy will doubtless be renting cots on her front stoop for the price of a bridal suite at the Waldorf-Astoria."

He transferred two of Mrs. Murphy's cats from his bed to Martin Brennan's. "Here, little man, is a couple of fur neckpieces for you. I grow my own." He laughed as he combed out his red beard. "And welcome it'll be on that wind-swept bit of prairie they're after naming the Great White City."

* * *

Conn was not greatly impressed by his first sight of the fairgrounds, except as a scene of the most colossal confusion. Some of the great buildings were completed and rose proudly in the gleaming whiteness of ornate plaster and stucco. Others were half finished, gaunt ribs of steel and timber cutting against the cold winter sky. Piles of lumber were scattered everywhere over ridges and mounds of frozen earth. Smoke rose from hundreds of small fires around which groups of workmen warmed themselves.

Massive statuary groups, their frail plaster of Paris covered by canvas, perched on flimsy-looking wooden legs; elaborate bridges spanned nonexistent canals. Mule teams by the hundreds struggled to haul dump carts and drays over the frozen ruts and hummocks.

Despite the cold, the frozen earth, and the biting wind from Lake Michigan, the work was going forward. The sound of hammers and saws, the chatter of riveters, and the monotonous cursing of the teamsters merged in an unceasing chorus.

As they stumbled over the uneven path Uncle Patrick explained a few of the features of the confused scene. "That long structure over there looking like a carbarn will be the Palace of Science and Industry when, and if, it's finished," he shouted. "That one the Fine Arts Building, that other the Transportation Building. These

swampy hollows will be lakes and lagoons beautified with statuary and fountains, Columbus and Venus rising from the foam, Tritons, Neptunes, and mermaids by the dozen.

Come spring, these blasted mountains of frozen prairie muck will be made into beautiful green lawns planted with rare and exotic plants and shrubbery."

"Likely," jeered Scrymer. "A regular 'Yde Park—I don't think."

"And this," went on Uncle Patrick as they picked their way along a path between two rows of assorted half-finished structures, "will be the great Midway. There will be shooting galleries, beer-gardens and sideshows and villages of every variety of strange and savage furriners; Japanese, Filipinos, Indians, Fijis, Egyptians, Eskimos—"

"Why don't they bring *them* along?" Scrymer interrupted. "Eskimos might feel at 'ome in this blinkin' climate."

"There'll be a German village, an Irish village, a bit of Old Vienna, maybe even a Cockney slum, Scrymer me lad, with its disgusting inhabitants in their native habitat. And straight ahead of us, dominating the whole scene, will rise the magnificent Ferris Wheel, the shining wonder of the century."

There certainly was no shining wonder visible at the moment, Conn thought—only a few laborers digging a hole. A small derrick was hauling up scoops of black prairie soil and emptying them into a line of waiting dump carts. The gang boss hailed Uncle Patrick and they all paused to peer into the hole, now about ten feet deep.

"Have you struck gold yet, Danny?" Uncle Patrick laughed.

"We have not," the boss answered. "We've struck ice and we've struck mud, we've struck water and we've struck quicksand—everything but the bones of a dinosaurus, and I'm expecting them any minute now."

"Well, you'd best be putting in some decent shoring there or you'll be having a cave-in and burying the bones of a lot of good Irishmen," Uncle Patrick said frowning. "You may have to go down fifty feet, by the looks of it, to strike a solid base. We can't be setting a couple of thousand tons of steel on a foundation floating on quicksand. What's more, there's seven more of these holes to be dug and Mr. Ferris wants to be pouring concrete in a week or two."

"Pour concrete?" Danny protested. "How can anybody pour concrete, let alone mix it, in this weather and it cold enough to freeze the marrow bones in a boiling stewpot?"

"Leave that to me and Mr. Ferris and get on with your digging," Uncle Patrick said.

He led his charges to a large shack built of corrugated iron and tarpaper. Inside was one large shedlike room where many draftsmen bent over tables covered with blueprints. Despite three huge glowing stoves they all wore hats and overcoats. A middle-aged man hurried over and greeted Uncle Patrick cordially, but in a lowered voice. He pointed to the far corner where three men were engaged in conversation.

"The boss is busy right now, Pat," he said. "But he'll be glad you're back. They're talking money. We're still short a hundred thousand dollars, but this looks promising. The fat one with the fur collar is Zillheimer, the big meatpacker. Rolling in it. The skinny one is Peabody, his lawyer and financial man."

So the third one must be the famous George Washington Gale Ferris, Conn thought, looking at him with interest. He did not appear especially unusual or impressive: of medium size, well but quietly dressed and rather young—in his mid-thirties, Conn guessed, although a heavy mustache made him look somewhat older. The only striking things about him were his keen, piercing, deepset eyes and his air of quiet but absolute confidence. "If he was to be telling you the world was square you'd be believing him—and he'd be right, likely," Conn thought.

Conn's eye fell on an elaborate construction of steel and wire on a nearby table. He nudged Uncle Patrick. "What is the squirrel cage yonder?" he asked.

Uncle Patrick rose and led him and Martin Brennan over to it.

"That, me boy," he said, "is an exact scale model of

the great wheel we're about to construct. These wee buglike things scattered around represent people. The little dollhouses are those great buildings we just passed outside, so you can judge the magnitude of it."

"I can see plain what you meant about its being like a bicycle wheel," Conn said. "The thin spokes of it and all. It looks strong, too."

"It is indeed," Uncle Patrick said, placing his great hand on the wheel. "As you can well see, it has two rims, one thirty feet inside of the other. Those two rims will be joined by girders and braces the like of a truss bridge, making it that strong you could take it off its two towers and roll it off across the prairie were you so minded—and had the strength."

The engineer who had greeted them turned to Martin Brennan. "We have some pretty husky work laid out for you, Brennan," he said. "This axle, for one thing. It will be forty-five feet long, thirty-three inches in diameter, the largest piece of steel ever forged in America. It will weigh something over forty-six tons and must be hoisted and placed in its bearings on top of those two towers. That's a lift of a hundred and forty-one feet from the ground. Can it be done?"

The little man studied the model thoughtfully for a few moments. "Give me the materials and a couple of small donkey engines and I'll lay it in its bearings as easy and gentle as you'd be putting a sleeping babe in the arms of its nurse," he said placidly.

"Good," the engineer laughed. "You have a confidence equal to Mr. Ferris's. He'll like you." They immediately plunged into a complicated discussion of cables, blocks, tackle, and weights and strains, while Conn continued to study the model of the great wheel.

He was so absorbed that he failed to notice the approach of Mr. Ferris and his two companions until Uncle Patrick hastily pulled him aside. As they passed, the boss gave Uncle Patrick a broad grin and a wink.

Mr. Zillheimer certainly looked rich, Conn thought. Everything about him spelled money: the fur-lined overcoat, the large pearl stickpin in the brocaded ascot tie, the gold-headed walking stick, and the heavy gold watch chain stretched across his ample paunch. Even the cigar that seemed grown into his ruddy face smelled expensive. Hands clasped behind his back, the pork king stared fixedly at the model, completely oblivious to Mr. Peabody's excited protests.

"But Mr. Ferris," the latter was saying. "The thing's impossible—ridiculous. Everyone I've talked to says it can't be done. Even if you should get it built, by some miracle, who would ever be idiotic enough to take a chance on riding it? Do you mean to tell me that sensible, responsible American people are going to pay good money to risk their lives on any such contraption as this?"

"I do," Mr. Ferris replied with a smile. "About fifteen thousand of them a day."

"Absurd," snapped Mr. Peabody. "There aren't that many fools in the country. The thing is bound to be a financial failure. You are proposing to spend four hundred thousand dollars, almost half a million, on this wild idea. You can't possibly get it built before the Fair is half over, if at all. Even if you should and there are a few fools willing to ride in it, you can't make back all that money in a few weeks."

Mr. Ferris continued to smile. "Here are the facts and figures, Mr. Peabody," he said quietly. "I will have the wheel completed, tested, and ready for business between the fifteenth and twentieth of June. Except for the committee's dilly-dallying, which has cost us six weeks, it would have been ready on May first, the opening day. However, June twentieth will give us slightly over four months to operate—one hundred and twenty-eight days, to be exact. We should average at least fifteen thousand passengers per day. At fifty cents each, that will mean seven thousand five hundred dollars each day. One hundred and twenty-eight days, therefore, will bring in a total of nine hundred and sixty thousand dollars, more than double the cost of the wheel. Deducting that original cost and our operating expenses, which will not be great, leaves at least four hundred thousand dollars—or a profit of one hundred per cent. I would consider that a rather handsome return."

"*If* you get the passengers, and *if* the fool thing doesn't collapse and *if* there are no accidents," shouted Mr. Peabody, "and a dozen other *ifs*. But how can you prove all these figures, what guarantees can you give?"

Mr. Ferris ceased to smile as he replied, "My word, Mr. Peabody. My word and my experience and my professional reputation, all of which are rather important to me. You must realize, as I certainly do, that if I have made the slightest error in any of my calculations, if there should be a mechanical failure of any kind, I would face complete ruin. I could never again find employment in the engineering profession, even to sharpen pencils. At every revolution of this wheel a thousand or more men, women and children will be entrusting their lives to the accuracy of my figures. That, to me, is a far heavier responsibility than any matter of dollars."

"That's all very well," Mr. Peabody began, "but—"

Mr. Zillheimer finally removed his gaze from the model and plucked the cigar from his mouth, rather in the manner of extracting a cork from a bottle. He silenced his adviser with a glance.

"All the success I've had," the pork magnate said,

"has come from doing what everybody else said was impossible. How much more money do you need, Ferris?"

"One hundred thousand dollars."

"Good, I'll take it. Shut up, Peabody. And one other thing, Mr. Ferris; I'd like to be a passenger on the first trip."

Mr. Ferris again smiled his youthful grin. "On the first official trip you will certainly be, Mr. Zillheimer, but I am afraid not on the *very* first trip. You see, in the case of every tunnel or bridge I have built, Mrs. Ferris and I have always made the first trip—alone. It is just an idea of ours, somewhat like the old-time royal food-taster. As you know, he always took the first bite or sip to make sure the dish contained no poison. We are the tasters for my constructions, and so far, I am glad to say, none of them has contained poison."

Mr. Zillheimer barked a short, sea-lion laugh. "The same with the Mrs. and me, too," he said. "We have for dinner first every new Zillheimer product. If it's no good, it's out. I stake my word and my reputation on every Zillheimer product. That's why people trust fellows like you and me. Good luck, Mr. Ferris. You'll have a check as soon as Peabody gets over his indigestion. I'm sending you a Zillheimer ham, too, and there won't anybody have to taste it first."

As soon as his visitors had left, Mr. Ferris hastened over and clapped Uncle Patrick happily on the back.

"Good to see you, Pat," he cried. "At last we are all straight financially and ready to go full steam ahead. And I see you have shanghaied some recruits from New York."

"I have indeed," Uncle Patrick replied, proudly introducing Martin Brennan and his crew. "The wee fellow here is a jaynius, I'm told. A master rigger five years in the best shipyards of Belfast, eight months with Webb in New York. He vouches for the two boxheads and, judging by the size of them, they ought to save us the use of a couple of derricks anyway. Scrymer there, the Duke of Limehouse, may not look like much, but he can put a running splice in steel cable so smooth you could be running your cheek over it and getting no more of a scratch than you would from a greased banana."

"Welcome, gentlemen," Mr. Ferris said. "Mr. Baldwin will take you over with tears of joy. He has been screaming for good riggers for two weeks now. And what about the young man, Pat? I seem to see a slight family resemblance there."

"My nephew," Uncle Patrick announced. "Cornelius Terence Kilroy. I have just rescued him from my brother who was all for making a lily-handed, pasty-faced clerk out of him. He's had some little experience in excavation, drainage, and concrete, and what he doesn't know I'll teach him—fast."

"Beginning at once," Mr. Ferris said. "Pat, I want you to take over those foundations, Danny isn't getting anywhere with them. Now that the money is assured I will wire all the steel companies to go into high gear. Our tower steel will be coming through very shortly, and we'll have to have something to set it on. I would like to start pouring concrete a week from today. You will strike solid bottom at thirty-five feet, which means that you have about five thousand cubic yards of muck to excavate. So fly at it."

"Yes *sir*," Uncle Patrick said with a happy grin. "You can begin to pour in six days, or my name is Zillheimer. Come, Conn me lad, this is no fiddling sewer ditch—you've got a man's job now."

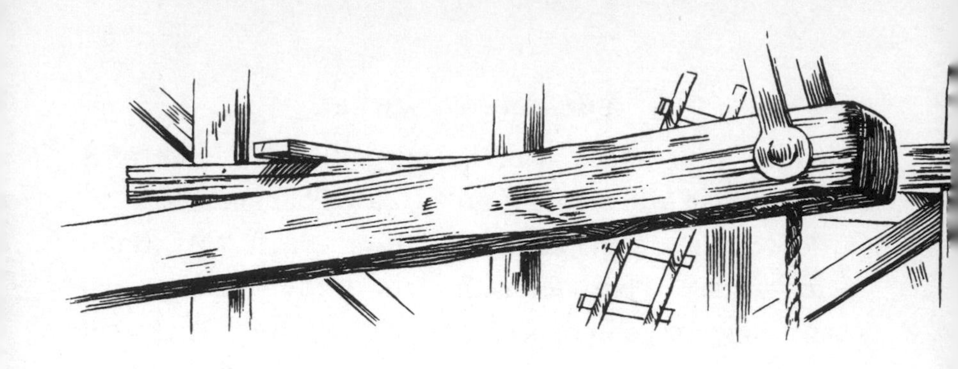

7

The next few weeks passed in a delirium of work. Some of the jobs in New York had been rather rushed and hectic, Conn thought, but compared to this one they seemed like restful vacations.

The moment they stepped out of Mr. Ferris's office, Uncle Patrick was transformed into a roaring, driving mass of energy. No wonder Mr. Ferris called him his right hand. He was hand, arm, feet, voice, and brawny back. He seemed to be in a half-dozen places at once: down in the hole, out among the dump carts, in the office, at the supply shed. Conn could keep track of him only by his bull voice and the flash of the red beard. Wherever he appeared and wherever his voice carried, the men became infected with his spirit. No need now for fires at which to warm themselves. Coats and mufflers were dis-

carded, and despite the biting cold the sweat began to flow.

Before they even reached the excavation Uncle Patrick was roaring orders. The derrick yanked out Danny's inadequate shoring. A squad of Swede carpenters appeared from nowhere and new planks and timbers were soon being assembled. Before long a veritable cofferdam, tight and massively cross-braced, was being driven down.

Another derrick arrived, the force of diggers was doubled, the dripping scoops of sand and muck came up faster and faster. The dump carts couldn't keep up with the flow, and more were sent for.

Conn was kept racing hither and yon, up and down the mud-caked ladders, to the supply shed, to the office. Now he was helping Danny boss the diggers, now helping the Swede timber workers, now holding a tape or plumb line for the engineers.

When darkness put a stop to their labors the excavation had reached a depth of sixteen feet, the new shoring of the twenty-foot-square hole was well and solidly built. Huge bonfires were left burning to thaw out the surface for the next two holes.

As they stumbled wearily across the cluttered waste of the fairgrounds they were joined by Martin Brennan and his crew.

"You've picked the wrong job, Conn me lad," Scrymer laughed. "Us riggers are working in a nice warm shed."

"And getting soft," Conn jeered. "Wait till you find yourself on the top of a derrick, like a monkey on a stick, with a wind off the lake whistling the snow around your ears and you'll wish you had some blood in your body instead of Thames water and porter."

The next day the pace, if anything, increased. A railroad spur was extended to the site. A huge concrete-mixer arrived and was unloaded. Conn and a gang knocked up a makeshift shelter of canvas and corrugated iron for it.

More laborers arrived, and work was begun on the next two holes. Scrymer and the two Norwegians rigged four more derricks. Steam-fitters came, bringing a boiler and a carload of piping. A maze of steampipes was laid beside the track where the sand would be dumped, heating pipes were hung in the shelter around the concrete-mixer, mains were laid to the excavation.

By noon of the fifth day Danny came to report that the first excavation had reached hardpan, at thirty-six feet.

"Mr. Ferris promised it at thirty-five feet," Uncle Patrick laughed. "Not a bad guess, but I'll tell him he must be getting senile. All right Danny. Clean it up." Then he bellowed for the steam-fitters.

By sunset, steampipes had been hung in the excavation and two huge Negroes had fired up the boiler. Conn and Uncle Patrick stood at the bottom of the hole looking up at the golden sky through a network of steampipes and crossbraces. The cold pipes clanged and banged as the steam began to circulate.

"Well, lad," Uncle Patrick said, "I promised to get you out of a sewer ditch and here I've got you down in a thirty-six-foot hole in the ground where you couldn't see the evening star without you had the neck of four giraffes on you. Cheer up, though. A month from now and you'll be thirty-six feet up in the steelwork and wishing to heaven you were back in your steam-heated excavation."

"How do you suppose Mr. Ferris knew that we'd strike solid bottom at thirty-five or thirty-six feet?" Conn wondered.

"How?" Uncle Patrick answered. "My boy, if I knew one quarter of the things are in that head of his, my brain would be splitting my skull into two halves."

At that moment Mr. Ferris's head appeared against the sky. "A nice clean solid job, Pat," he called down. "And two days ahead of schedule. About what I'd expected of you. Don't let that young nephew push you too hard though. Remember you're not as young as you once were." He smiled happily as Uncle Patrick's outraged bellow came up from below and turned to his companion.

"You can start pouring tomorrow, Walker," he said. "And keep it going until they're all finished. Put on a night shift. Pat will keep one hole ahead of you if he has to dig them himself."

Shortly after sunrise the next morning the concrete-mixer was rumbling and grinding steadily. Two processions of wheelbarrows moved unceasingly up the wooden ramp carrying sand and stone. Four gigantic Negroes, their faces already gray with dust, spelled each other, dumping sacks of cement into the mixer's insatiable maw. From a short inclined trough a stream of wet concrete ran and dripped and plopped into the depths of the great square hole.

To Conn looking at the small inadequate stream it seemed impossible that the hole would ever be filled, but already the bottom was covered and the pudding-like gray tide was starting almost imperceptibly to creep up the hissing steampipes. Uncle Patrick brought Danny over to look.

"There now, Danny," he said. "Do you see how Mr. Ferris and me work concrete in freezing weather? 'Tis only child's play, this. When you're on a river bottom with thirty feet of water over your head and an air pressure on you would crack the drums in your ears, then you're doing a man's work. Now get back to your digging and let's hear no more talk about how things can't be done."

At sunset a night shift of laborers came on; kerosene flares were set around here and there to light the work. The procession of wheelbarrows continued without interruption, the mixer ground and rumbled, the stream of concrete plopped steadily into the hole.

When they returned next morning the hole was a third filled and four heavy twisted-steel rods were being hung from the cross braces. The engineers with transit and tape checked their placing with the greatest care.

"Anchor bolts," Uncle Patrick explained. "With them buried in the concrete and bolted to each leg our towers ought to stand up to any gale that ever blew and an earthquake or two thrown in."

The work went on systematically now. There came a warm rain that turned the site into a sea of mud. It was followed by a spell of zero cold that turned the mud into iron-hard ruts and hummocks, but the steampipes kept the sand dry and unfrozen, the concrete setting properly. As each foundation was finished the mixer was shifted to the next hole and the pouring continued almost without interruption.

Days stretched into weeks unnoticed; Conn had lost all track of time. At night he ate Mrs. Murphy's good food and staggered up to bed. There were no Sundays off, for there could be no stop in the concrete pouring. There was no time to talk with Martin Brennan or even Uncle Patrick except for short consultations on the work. He did realize that the days were growing a bit longer, but that meant only longer hours of labor, for their working day was from sunrise to sunset.

It came as a sudden surprise when one afternoon Uncle

Patrick heaved himself up out of the eighth excavation, wiped his hands on his muddy overalls, and announced, "Well, laddie, there goes the last scoopful of muck. Our sewer work is done. Now let's clean up this mess."

Half the diggers were let go, and Conn set the rest to straightening up. Two days later he and his gang suddenly ceased their labors, startled by a strange stillness. The concrete-mixer had stopped!

The fireman dumped his fire, the engineer tied down the whistle. The shrill blast brought the draftsmen, the riggers, and the rest crowding from the sheds. As the scream of the whistle died away in a last watery gurgle, Mr. Ferris himself came out to congratulate Uncle Patrick.

"Well done, Pat," he said. "And a week ahead of schedule. You'd better take a couple of days off, you and your nephew both. You deserve it."

The next day, coming over to collect some pay, Uncle Patrick and Conn surveyed the now deserted scene. The sand pile and its pipes, the small mountain of crushed stone were all gone. The concrete-mixer had been loaded on a flatcar and hauled away. Left-over planks and timbers were neatly stacked. Only the steam-boiler and its lone Negro fireman remained; the pipes buried in the foundations would be kept hot for some days still.

The result of the previous weeks of bustling labor did

not look impressive: only eight evenly placed slabs of concrete that might have been chicken-house floors, each with four heavy bolts protruding a foot or more.

"It doesn't look like much for all that work," Conn said.

"It does not," Uncle Patrick agreed, lighting his pipe. "Unless you know what's underground. Over four thousand yards of concrete. Eight great monoliths, the way scientific men of future ages may be digging them up and wondering what strange race of people buried them there and why. They'll little guess that it was all for the amusement of the public at fifty cents a ride."

Conn enjoyed the short rest. He had seen nothing at all of Chicago, so Uncle Patrick showed him the city, which did not impress him very favorably. Compared to New York it seemed quite crude and garish. And the ever-present aroma of the stockyards and slaughterhouses was far from pleasant. He bought a few clothes and a fur cap. He also purchased a buffalo robe to send to Uncle Michael; the shops were full of them at ridiculously low prices.

With considerable struggle he managed to write quite a long letter to his cousin Agnes. He would have liked to send one to Trudy, too. The thought of her blue eyes, serious and wide with trust as she said, "You will come,

it is your fortune,'' had lain warm in his memory ever since that last evening at sea. But he did not know her address, even her last name. He felt quite sure that the Post Office Department, wonderful though it was, could hardly cope with a letter addressed simply to *Miss Trudy, Wisconsin*.

On Monday they reported back for work. Conn still could not get used to the deserted air of the place; he had a sinking feeling that the whole project had fallen through. The office shack was even more forlorn. Most of the engineers and draftsmen were gone. Mr. Ferris sat in solitary meditation before one of the glowing stoves, his hat on the back of his head, his feet propped on a box.

''Welcome, Pat,'' he said. ''All's quiet along the Midway. The lull before the storm, you might say. I have sent most of the boys over to Detroit to check on the steelwork as it is fabricated. You might go along and keep an eye on things for a while.

"I want every piece of steel that goes into this construction checked and rechecked for accuracy, every piece clearly marked and numbered. I have given them a schedule for shipments and want it carried out to the hour. We can't be sorting out mixed-up lots of steel here in three feet of snow or mud. We can't waste time reaming out inaccurately placed bolt holes or straightening bent rods or girders.

"We shall have four times more steel to erect than there is in the Niagara Falls Bridge. It took them three years to build that and we will have exactly five months. It will take speed—and accuracy."

"I'll take the next train," said Uncle Patrick, "and I promise you this, Mr. Ferris. For every sixteenth of an inch of error you find in that steel you can slice that much off the end of my nose."

He grabbed up his hat and rushed out. Mr. Ferris, lost in thought, resumed his contemplation of the glowing stove.

"Is there anything you'd want me to be doing, Mr. Ferris?" Conn finally asked.

"Nothing special," his employer replied. "Lulls like this are very infrequent in this profession. Enjoy it while you can. Sit down a while."

He lit a cigar and leaned back in his chair. For some time he talked quietly of his work; of the bridges and tunnels and railroads he had built, of his research work with the steel companies.

"It all becomes more or less routine after a while, Conn," he said. "The problems pretty much the same. This wheel thing is a delightful change for me, fun really, something different. Yet it is not a ridiculous notion, a Ferris's Folly, as many contend. Every detail of it is based on the soundest engineering principles. It is completely practical and will be just as safe as any steel bridge or building ever built. It cannot fail to operate successfully. Yet just because it is something that has never been done before it has met with nothing but opposition, timidity, and ridicule."

"I'd hate to be the man would speak disparagement of it in earshot of Uncle Patrick," Conn said, with a grin.

Mr. Ferris laughed. "I would too," he said. "He's a grand man, your uncle, I don't know how I would get along without him. But tell me about yourself. How do you like working with us?"

So Conn told him about his life in Ireland, about Uncle Michael's letter, and about the work in New York. Mr. Ferris listened with such sympathetic attention that he even told, somewhat hesitantly, of Aunt Honora's prophecy.

"Wouldn't you think it a strange thing, Mr. Ferris," he asked, "her to be telling me about riding the greatest wheel in the world and now me being here to help build it and all?"

Mr. Ferris threw his cigar into the stove and watched the momentary flare.

"Very remarkable," he said finally, "remarkable and wonderful. But it doesn't astonish me especially. It may surprise you, Conn, but you see we engineers, supposedly so hard-boiled and practical, are great dealers in dreams and visions. As much so as poets and artists. For everything we build is first only a dream—then we make the dream come true. Instead of brush or pen we do it with steel and concrete, with slide-rule and tape and transit, bolts and rivets—but first was the dream.

"Out there, right now, there is just a messy field of frozen mud and some slabs of concrete. But there is also a vision. Close your eyes and think hard and you can see it—the great towering wheel turning slowly, majestically, soundlessly. Lifting people up for a little while into the clear upper air, out of the dust and noise of their everyday existence. Giving them a glimpse of wider horizons than they have ever known—perhaps a closer sight of the evening star. I wonder if Ferris's Folly is as foolish as it seems, to some?"

Conn had no answer, but he began to understand how Uncle Patrick was bewitched by the man.

8

For Conn the next two weeks were almost a vacation. He was supposed to be helping Martin Brennan and his crew, but they needed little help. Martin was busy with his preparations for raising the great axle when the towers were completed. He had ordered four of the biggest steel blocks ever made and a mile or so of cable. There were slings, hooks, chains, and toggles to be procured, new winches to be arranged for. Martin had no time to be bothered with him. Conn did help Scrymer and the two Norwegians rig several derricks and gin poles to handle the steel when it should arrive, but there was still considerable time to wander about the fairgrounds and watch the feverish activity visible everywhere.

In his wanderings he finally came across the German Village on the midway. It was to be a replica of a corner of a medieval German town—cobbled streets, half-timbered houses, the great gate of an ancient castle. Here, strangely enough, there was no haste or bustle. The stolid German artisans—carpenters, masons, ironworkers—went about their tasks slowly and methodically. Most of the buildings were almost completed, and Conn was astonished to find that they were really built as though for all time, not mere fabrications of lath and plaster.

He expressed his surprise to one of the carpenters who was eating his lunch. The man sliced off a large slab of sausage and offered it to Conn. He shrugged and glanced at him quizzically. "How else?" he asked. "There iss only one way—the right way. To build, you build goot."

His accent and his blue eyes reminded Conn of Trudy. "Do you know anything about Wisconsin?" he asked.

"Witsconsin? Jah, sure. I am from Witsconsin."

"Would you be knowing a man named Otto, a German fellow?" Conn asked. "He has cows and makes cheese."

The other laughed and cut off another slice of sausage. "Witsconsin is a big state," he said. "There are many Germans. Most have cows, most make cheese. Many are named Otto. What is the rest of his name?"

"I don't know," Conn confessed. "Only he's an uncle of somebody I met on the boat. Her name is Trudy."

"In Witsconsin are many Trudys, too. You should go to Witsconsin and look."

"Maybe I will some time," Conn said. "After we've finished the great wheel."

"You work on that wheel? The Ferris Folly wheel?" The carpenter shook his head sadly. "It will not work. Too quick builded. It will fall down. In Germany we would build it right."

"Would you indeed?" Conn flared. "I'm telling you now, mister, anything Mr. Ferris is building will be built right."

Undisturbed, the other finished his lunch, closed his lunch pail, and put it away carefully. He picked up an oak plank on which he had been working, sighted along its edge, and marked a few high spots with his pencil.

"Jah," he said placidly. "It will collapse and you will be killed. Too bad."

Conn wandered over to Old Vienna, another attraction that was being slowly and methodically constructed in the German way. He talked with many of the workmen, always ending with questions about Uncle Otto and Trudy. Plenty of them knew plenty of Ottos, but none with a niece named Trudy. Plenty of them knew plenty of Trudys, but none with an Uncle Otto. "You should wait," one carpenter advised. "In the summer all Witsconsin will come to the fair. You will find them then."

For the first time Conn began to wonder what would happen in the spring when the wheel was finished. He had supposed vaguely that he would go on with Uncle Patrick and Mr. Ferris to some other big job; he knew they were both pleased with his work, that they would want him. But now he wasn't so sure that he wanted to move on. Oh well, he'd see. After all the wheel wasn't finished yet; it was hardly begun.

That night at Mrs. Murphy's he found a letter from Cousin Agnes:

Dear Cousin Connie,

We were all that glad to hear from you. We have been reading in the papers about Mr. Ferris's great wheel, but Papa and all his friends say it will never work. Some say it will never be finished, that it will collapse, but I pray it will not because that would be a great danger to you and Uncle Patrick. It makes me very fearful to think of you working at those great heights and I hope you will be careful. Please stay on the ground as much as you can.

Now I will tell you a great secret but you must not breathe a word of it to anyone. Mamma and Stella and I are going to begin to work on Papa to take us to the Fair this summer, instead of that tiresome old Brighton Beach. Won't that be exciting? Lots of our friends are planning to go but Papa says it is just a waste of money. He says that there will not be much to see that is worth while and he wouldn't ride on the Ferris Wheel if you paid him. He says that he can't see why all this great Fair is being made to honor Columbus who was only an Italian sailor anyway. If it was for Robert Emmet or George Washington there'd be some sense to it he says.

But we will bring him around, never fear, and by the time our trunks are packed he will think it was all his idea.

I am glad to know that you find your muffler a comfort. Chicago must be awfully cold. I am knitting you some woolen socks now, but I am afraid they will take as long to make as your great wheel.

Papa says to tell you that Tommy Glynn is doing pretty well, but he can never take your place. He can't with me either, although he would like to.

Your affectionate cousin,

Agnes.

Conn chuckled as he read it. He could well imagine the subtle but irresistible "working on" that Uncle Michael was in for. Agnes was pretty and attractive, there was no denying that, but if she had decided they were going to the Fair—they were going to the Fair. Uncle Michael might just as well go out and buy their tickets to Chicago right now.

He decided to answer her at once, while things were leisurely. Once the steel arrived, there would be no time for letter-writing or anything else. He lit the gas, sharpened a pencil, and squared away before a blank sheet of paper.

Outside, framed by Mrs. Murphy's stiffly starched lace

curtains, the evening sky shone coldly, sharply etched by the stark timbers of unfinished buildings. Here and there puffs of blue steam showed where donkey engines still labored.

Suddenly the evening star was there. It seemed higher than usual and steadier. It did not twinkle and beckon, but shone down peacefully, restfully. It was so clear that it seemed not like a pinprick in the curtain of the sky, but as though it were projected forward in space, hanging directly over the fairgrounds.

Conn glanced down and was surprised to find that he had begun his letter *Dear Trudy*. Oh well, Agnes would have to wait a while. He might as well go on with this even though it couldn't be mailed. It was easier to write what you thought if it wasn't going to be mailed, or read.

Dear Miss Trudy,

I'm thinking it's a grand fortune my Aunt Honora read me the way I've followed the evening star here to Chicago and now it looks so close I could amost lean out the window and give it a poke with a buggy whip. Maybe it is over Wisconsin but I do not know what direction that would be. Anyway it doesn't seem to call me to be ever moving to the west any more, so perhaps I have come far enough.

I'm wondering if you'll ever be looking at it from there in Wisconsin, or have you forgotten about my Aunt Honora and her fortune and about me too—the redheaded lad was on the City of Bristol crossing the ocean?

Well I am here in Chicago helping my Uncle Patrick build the great Ferris Wheel and when it's finished I'll ride it and that will end the fortune, for I'll have rode the greatest wheel in all the world the way it said.

Martin Brennan, the wee crooked man was on the boat is here too. He is my best friend. I hope that there are no Indians in Wisconsin and that you are all well. I can not mail this for I do not have your address, but I will keep it until I do.

Yours truly,

Cornelius Terence Kilroy.

He put it in an envelope and tucked it away in his bureau drawer under his best Sunday shirt, which so far he had not had an opportunity to wear.

Just as he was going to bed, Uncle Patrick came bursting in. He greeted Conn boisterously, threw his bag in the corner, yawned, and stretched mightily.

"Well lad," he roared, "your leisure days are over. Our first load of steel will be here in the morning."

When they reached the site next morning they found several flatcars piled high with massive steel girders waiting on the siding. There was also a gang of construction workers, brought from one of Mr. Ferris's newly completed bridges.

These men were an entirely new breed to Conn—lean and rangy, mostly, hard-bitten and capable and with a devil-may-care air about them that reminded Conn a bit of the cowboys he'd seen around the stockyards. They wore leather gauntlets and heavy belts from which dangled various tools that clanged as they walked. They all had Uncle Patrick's easy, cat-like tread.

Uncle Patrick was greeted with whoops and handshakes and much hilarious backslapping. One odd-looking man, obviously their boss, hailed him with special warmth. He was a tall, spare, middle-aged individual, black-bearded, heavily lined, and with eyes set deep under bushy brows. His long hair fell to the collar of a gray, brass-buttoned overcoat. He wore a broad-brimmed gray hat rakishly pinned up on one side and black kid gloves, and carried a silver-mounted walking stick. His deep voice bore a strong southern accent as he greeted Uncle Patrick with old-time courtesy.

"Mr. Giblin," he cried. "We meet again. You are a sight for sore eyes, suh. It is a pleasure to be once more engaged with you on another of Mr. Ferris's projects."

"Stonewall Jackson, you old Rebel," shouted Uncle Patrick. "It's famished I've been for a look at you. Welcome to the White City and a job worthy of your talents." He called Conn over.

"Conn me lad," he said, "meet my old friend General Jackson, late Captain of Engineers, Army of the Confederacy; the best steel construction boss, barring myself, either side of the Mississippi River. General, my nephew, Cornelius Terence Kilroy."

"A pleasure, suh," the man said, gravely extending his hand. "I trust I will have the pleasure of seeing more of you. And now, gentlemen, if you will excuse me, I believe there is work to be done."

He bowed, wheeled smartly, and strode off toward the railroad siding, followed by his grinning gang. Like well-drilled soldiers they swarmed over the laden cars. Donkeymen started the winches, derricks creaked, blocks rattled, huge girders rose, swung, and were gently lowered to heavy timber skids laid out upon the frozen ground.

The ex-Confederate, casually smoking a thin cheroot, appeared lazy and relaxed, but his deep-set eyes were everywhere. Occasionally he pointed with his walking stick and rasped out a sharp order which was carried out with military precision. The steelwork was being laid out as exactly as a shop-counter display.

"He wouldn't really be the great General Stonewall Jackson, now, would he, Uncle Patrick?" Conn asked, watching the unloading with awe.

Uncle Patrick roared with laughter. "Hardly, you

young greenhorn, and him dead some thirty years ago in the great war,'' he chortled. ''You'll be learning that any southerner of the name of Jackson gets to be called Stonewall or General by the way of a nickname. He's a real veteran, though, and a fine educated gentleman. Don't ever let yourself be deceived by his polite manners, either. I've seen him set down a drunken river-front bully by the mere glance of his eye and that gentle tongue of his'll flay the hide off a shirker quicker than any mule skinner's lash. He's a driver, but every man on the job would work his heart out to please him.'' He walked over to join Mr. Ferris and the General, who were now in consultation.

''Pat,'' Mr. Ferris said. ''I want you to take charge of the north tower, Jackson the south. Now remember, speed is of great importance, but safety of far greater. Many thousands of lives will depend on your thoroughness. One missing bolt, one faulty fastening might spell a disaster too awful to contemplate. I am depending on you two to see to it that there is no possibility of one. As to speed—while this is not to be considered as exactly a race, there *will* be an extra day's pay for the crew whose tower is topped out first.''

''You may set your mind at rest, suh,'' General Jackson said. ''Safety will never be sacrificed to speed. And now, Mr. Giblin, you have the honor of first choice.''

"Dan Sullivan," Uncle Patrick said promptly.

"Slim Tolliver."

"Joe Blakeslee."

And so General Jackson and Uncle Patrick began picking their crews with all the eagerness of two lads choosing sides for a game of shinny.

That night Conn added a postscript to his letter:

Dear Trudy,

The first of the steel came today and tomorrow we begin work on the two great towers that will hold the Wheel. So I may not have any great time to be writing you, but I can be thinking. Uncle Patrick chose me to be on his crew. I don't know why, for I've had little experience in this work, but I'll try hard to learn.

Cornelius.

9

Maybe this wasn't exactly a race, Conn thought, but it certainly wasn't any dawdling match either. He leaned far out, held only by his safety belt, caught the end of a swinging girder, and wrestled it into place. As the bolt holes lined up, Pop Jenks, his partner, drove the long, pointed handle of his spud wrench through two of them, locking the girder to the corner plate. Conn already had a bolt out of the sack at his waist. He shot it through a hole, spun the nut on and drew it tight with a grunt as he heaved his whole weight on the wrench handle.

There were twelve holes; Conn and Pop Jenks each shot six bolts through, spun and tightened the nuts in perfect unison. Almost simultaneously each unhooked a hammer from his belt, drew out a punch, and proceeded to lock his nuts with a deep punch mark driven where thread and nut met. From the other end of the girder they could hear the clanging blows as their opposite partners locked their nuts.

Unconsciously they both glanced across at the south tower, thirty feet away, and noted with satisfaction that they were a bit ahead. The corresponding girder for the south tower's crew was just starting up from the ground. But there was no time for gloating; already a new beam was dangling before their faces. Conn hauled it into place and again they started bolting up.

It seemed incredible that only three weeks ago he had never been off the ground save for an occasional climb in the rigging of a ship with Martin Brennan. Three weeks ago he had not known a lattice girder from an I-beam, a spud wrench from a reamer. And here he was, eighty feet in the air, sitting back on his safety as much at home as if he'd been in an easy chair and holding up his end with Pop Jenks, one of the best steel men in the country.

It was Jenks' steadiness and experience that had made Uncle Patrick pick him to be Conn's partner and teacher. It was on the very first day of construction, when the enormous corner beams were being bolted to the concrete foundations, that Uncle Patrick had led him over to where Jenks was working.

"Pop," Uncle Patrick had said. "This is my nephew Conn Kilroy. He's green as the fields of Erin, but he's going to be a steel man and you're going to teach him—fast. He'll be a burden to you for a while, but you can do with a bit handicap anyhow. You're too fast for the rest."

Jenks looked Conn over for some time. When he finally spoke, it was with a slow southern drawl. "Reckon I've tackled tougher jobs," he said. He grinned broadly as his gaze settled on Conn's mop of flaming hair. "Leastwise I'll know where he's at, come a foggy day." He handed Conn a long-handled wrench and indicated a bag of bolts. "All right, son," he said. "Bolt up that plate."

Conn rather clumsily inserted a row of bolts, carefully screwed the nuts on, then tightened them with the wrench. With a smile his instructor took the wrench from him and picked up a handful of bolts. Quickly he shot one through a hole, placed a nut on it and flicked it with thumb and finger. The nut spun down the shank of the bolt, bringing up sharply against the plate. Almost before it stopped the wrench caught it and Jenks threw his whole weight on the long handle. He fitted the wrench to one of Conn's nuts and swung on it. The nut turned a full half-revolution.

"See, son?" he said. "They want to be tight, they're not decorations. Heave your weight on 'em till you grunt. And spin your nut down, saves time. If you get a bad nut don't fiddle with it. Drop it, only make sure there's nobody underneath. From a hundred feet one of 'em'll go through a man's head quicker'n the thought of pay day. Now do it right."

Conn did it, not quickly or skillfully, but right. Under Jenks's patient, watchful teaching he learned in days what others took months to master. Before long he ceased to be a burden to his partner; now they worked on almost equal terms.

"This here's the best way to begin," Pop said. "Starting at the bottom and working up as the tower grows, you won't notice the height so much. Funny thing about height, some fellers never can take it. 'Taint a matter of nerve, either.

"Take my brother Bud there, working on the ground crew now. He's afraid of nothing on earth—long as it's *on* the earth. Started out to be a steel man and was getting on fine. We were building one of Mr. Ferris's bridges down in West Virginia, 'bout a hundred feet up over a river. All of a sudden one day, fer no reason at all he froze onto a brace and couldn't move. I went over and asks him what's the matter and he couldn't answer. Just hung on there, white as a sheet, eyes glassy and sweat running down his face, spite of it was a cold day.

"I wrapped so many ropes around him he looked like a cocoon and hitched him onto a derrick sling to lower him down, but it took two of us to pry his hands loose one finger at a time, using our spud wrenches to do it.

Once he was on the ground he was all right, but even now he can't as much as climb a stepladder. Ever feel one of them spells coming on, son, just be sure your safety's fastened to something solid—and holler."

Luckily Conn was not bothered by heights. He soon learned to trust his safety belt completely. With his feet firmly planted against an upright column he was able to lean easily out and back, his arms and hands free to work, the broad leather strap comfortingly snug about his hips.

There was something wonderfully exhilarating about working at a height. The air seemed clearer, the sunlight brighter. Each day as the tower went up their view broadened, the horizon retreated farther and farther. Soon they were above the surrounding buildings, all Chicago spread out before them, the vast frozen wastes of Lake Michigan stretching as far to the north and east as they could see.

To the south and west there were limitless miles of flat, snow-covered farm-land, checkered by straight fence lines and square wood lots. Railroads radiated in every direction like a huge spider web with Chicago as its center. He could see dark trains creeping, spewing streamers of black smoke.

"Which way would be Wisconsin?" Conn asked his partner.

"Up along the lake shore. 'Bout forty miles or so north, I reckon," Pop answered. "Thinkin' of goin' there?"

"I might, some day."

But there was little time for admiring the view or thinking about Wisconsin. It was becoming a real race now between the two tower crews. Rivalry was keen too between the ground crews as they snaked and skidded the heavy girders from the siding to the towers. The prize of an extra day's pay was of little importance; most of them were making good money, nine to twelve dollars a week. It was purely pride and loyalty to their bosses that drove them.

Nothing could have been a greater contrast than the methods of these two. There was Uncle Patrick, roaring and shouting, now up a tower, now heaving on a crowbar, now lending his weight on a rope, hat off, red beard bristling with energy. And on the other hand Stonewall Jackson, negligently smoking his slender cheroot, never hurrying, seldom speaking, pointing now and then with his walking stick, his black kid gloves never soiled by the touch of rope or cable.

Yet both methods seemed to work equally well, for the two towers rose with incredible speed, but absolute uniformity. Neither side could gain an inch. The raked corner beams were coming closer and closer together, the cross girders were shorter, the men almost got in one another's way as the space became more limited.

Then one day Conn was suddenly transfixed by an

unearthly wailing scream. His breath caught, prickles ran up and down his spine. Someone must have fallen.

Almost at the same moment Pop Jenks set up a mighty clanging, banging the long handle of his spud wrench against a girder. "Topped out!" he roared, and far below they could hear it echoed by Uncle Patrick's bellow.

Still the Rebel yells continued, rising higher and more piercing even than the donkey-engine whistles which now joined the din. On the ground they could see a small group arguing and gesticulating, Mr. Ferris among them. They saw General Jackson and Uncle Patrick shaking hands. Then in a momentary lull Uncle Patrick's roar came up again.

"A dead heat," he shouted. "All bets off. A day's pay for everybody. Knock off!"

Whooping and shouting, boasting and arguing, the tower crews came down, five or six men clinging to a derrick sling, others sliding down tie rods or climbing down the lattice girders.

The towers were finished.

Conn enjoyed the afternoon off. He wandered about the fairgrounds where the activity was increasing daily. He talked with the workers at the German Village and Old Vienna. He looked at the various state buildings which were rapidly nearing completion; Pennsylvania's reproduction of Independence Hall, New York State's huge monstrosity, the beautiful Virginia Building. He looked in at the Irish Village and was disappointed to find that the carpenters were all Swedes.

Back home at Mrs. Murphy's, he started to write to Agnes. He really should, he thought, but there didn't seem to be much to say. He ought to express interest in their coming visit to Chicago, but he probably wouldn't be here then, so what did it matter?

He wrote:

Dear Trudy,

The towers are finished and now we'll have the great wheel to build. It was fun working on them, especially high up, the way I could see up the lake almost to Wisconsin. Sure America is a fine big country. Everywhere I could look is miles and miles of farms, little houses and big barns. I could see cows too, big herds of them, the like of Wisconsin maybe.

I like cows, they're quiet decent animals with kind hearts to them. At home I liked the red cow fine, the way she'd give more milk for me than for anyone else. And in winter when the nights were cold her bit stable was always that warm. I'd go there sometimes for the comfort of it.

Did you know of a Christmas Eve at midnight they will face to the east and kneel? I told my Cousin Agnes that last Christmas and she said it was only a silly old superstition, but it is not. It is true, for I have seen it with my own two eyes.

The days are getting longer now and not so cold. Today we saw great flocks of wild geese flying north, high in the sky. They fly in strange straight lines like the geometry angles Father Riley was always drawing for us that I never could understand. The voices of them sound like lads playing at hurley in a village far off.

Your friend,

Conn.

Next day the massive lower halves of the bearings were hoisted and set in place on the towers. Martin Brennan and his crew, with a few skilled steelworkers, busied themselves bolting and bracing two squatty, thick-armed derricks to the tower tops. Martin was now the man of the hour, for the great shaft was due at any time, and hoisting it was his responsibility. The four huge blocks, his pride and joy, were hung from the derricks. Two steam winches fitted with enormous drums were brought up and securely anchored near the towers. The cables were rigged, huge collars and slings were readied.

Martin scuttled around with his crabwise gait, inspecting everything. The gigantic Norwegians worked silently. Scrymer, whistling tunelessly through the gap left by his missing teeth, performed prodigies of beautiful splicing.

In the midst of all this activity the shrill blast of a switch engine signaled the arrival of the shaft. It was mounted on two of the heaviest flatcars obtainable. Large signs proclaimed that it was the largest forging ever made in America, that it was produced by the Bethlehem Iron Company and was destined for the World's Columbian Exposition at Chicago. Its slow journey from Pennsylvania had been in the nature of a triumphal progress.

It *was* impressive, Conn thought—forty-five feet of gleaming steel the diameter of a flour barrel. Its seventeen-inch bore gave it the look of a cannon for a war of giants. And heavy! It took a full day of sweating and straining by all the steelworkers, or roaring and exhortation by Uncle Patrick to get it unloaded and in place.

Next morning an unnatural air of quiet and tension hung over the job. The great gleaming shaft lay on enormous wooden chocks. Near each end, heavy collars and cables bound it to the lower blocks.

Mr. Ferris called to Uncle Patrick, "I want everyone well away from under the towers, Pat. Nothing can go wrong I'm sure, but—"

No one showed any inclination to linger, everyone moved well back, leaving only Uncle Patrick, midway between the two towers, and Martin Brennan who was busily making last-minute inspections. The boilers began popping off steam, the donkeymen fingered their levers.

Finally Martin straightened up and called quietly, "All right, Mr. Giblin. Take it away, and keep it level, please."

Uncle Patrick stretched his arms wide; his hands moved gently up and down. The donkeymen moved their levers slightly and the little engines began their busy chuffing. Uncle Patrick's hands moved faster, the engines stepped up their pace, spewing clouds of steam into thc cold air. The great drums revolved slowly and steadily.

With the great lengths of cable used, it required several moments to take up the slack and the stretch. The sheaves turned in the blocks, the cables grew straight and taut, but the huge shaft remained still, heavy, solid, seemingly immovable.

Conn's heart was pounding, his eyes fixed on the great wooden chocks on which the shaft rested. Suddenly a strip of light appeared, a steadily widening space opened up.

The shaft was rising!

At almost the same moment he was aware of a sharp exclamation of rage from General Jackson. "The little idiot," he snapped.

Then Conn saw Martin Brennan, a long spouted oilcan in one hand, scrambling aboard the shaft. At the same time Scrymer, similarly armed, leaped up on the other end. Holding to the huge sling with one hand, Martin, stretching on tiptoe, reached up and squirted a few unnecessary drops of oil on the bearings of the block. Then he sat down, fished out his pipe, and began to load it.

The General started forward, his mouth opening to shout, but Mr. Ferris laid a restraining hand on his arm. "The little man has faith," he said quietly. "Let him enjoy his small moment of triumph."

Uncle Patrick's hands fluttered faster, the little engines' chuffing became a steady purr. The Negro firemen scattered coal and sliced their fires expertly, keeping an even pressure. The shaft rose steadily, slowly—like the tide rising up the rocks on Kilda Point, Conn thought.

Martin Brennan had his pipe lit now. Arm hooked through the heavy sling, he settled back for the long slow climb. Scrymer crossed his knees, tilted back his hat, and burst into song.

'Oo threw the overalls in Mrs. Murphy's CHOWder?
Nobody answered so they shouted all the LOUder.
It's a dirty Irish trick and I can lick the Mick
'Oo threw the overalls into the C-H-O-W-W-W-der.

The tension eased. Someone laughed; General Jackson relit his cheroot. The men shifted their feet, bit off fresh chews of tobacco, joked and talked quietly. Conn, suddenly aware that his nails were cutting the flesh, relaxed his clenched fists. Only Uncle Patrick remained rigid, his

RL

eyes fixed on the slowly ascending shaft, arms outstretched, hands gently fluttering.

The slow, deliberate ascent took a full hour. Conn couldn't have told whether it was ten minutes or two days. Scrymer had been endlessly singing.

Drill ye tarriers drill,
Drill ye tarriers drill,
For it's work all day
For the sugar in your tay,
Drill ye tarriers drill.
Drill ye—

He suddenly broke off as the shaft reached a point a few inches higher than the bearings. Uncle Patrick's hands stiffened; the engines sighed wearily and were still.

Martin and Scrymer took up the signaling. As they waved their long oilcans the stubby derricks turned slightly until the great shaft was directly over the bearings. Simultaneously both spouts pointed straight downward. Uncle Patrick's hands stroked the air gently, the reversed engines chuffed quietly, and softly as a lighting butterfly the heavy shaft settled into the waiting cradle of its bearings. As the huge slings slackened, Scrymer snatched off his hat and scaled it into the air. Martin Brennan stepped down to the tower top as though alighting from a coach-and-four. The donkeymen blew jubilant blasts of their whistles.

Conn discovered that his neck was painfully stiff, his back aching. Uncle Patrick's bellow rose to the skies. "Scrymer, you blithering Cockney songbird," he roared, "come down off of that tower till I take you apart and feed you to the seagulls."

Scrymer thumbed his nose, the men laughed and busied themselves hauling over the upper halves of the bearing blocks. By quitting time that evening they had been raised and bolted down in place.

"Well, there's your axle, Mr. Giblin," Martin said as they gazed up at the huge shaft black against the sunset sky. "Now all you've got to do is hang a wheel on it."

10

"The flowers that bloom in the spring, trar lar," sang Scrymer as they picked their way across the fairgrounds the next day.

There was reason for song, for, all unnoticed, spring had crept upon them. The wandering breeze from the southwest was positively balmy, laden with vague scents of barns and cattle, wet earth and melting snow.

Like ants called from their runs by the first mild days, workers by the thousands swarmed over the grounds. Mule-drawn scrapers, scoops, and harrows were attacking the great mounds of black prairie soil, spreading it out into smoothly graded lawns. Drays laden with shrubs and plants struggled through the soft earth. Gleaming white plaster sculptures were being rolled out and placed

on their foundations. The lagoons were filling with water. Scrap lumber and rubbish were burning in a hundred bonfires.

High above everything else rose the two towers, dominating the whole scenc. They looked very different, now that they were connected by the wheel's great shaft. Martin Brennan was preparing to hoist the spiders—the huge cast-iron hubs to which the spokes of the wheel would be attached. Since they were in sections that weighed but five tons or so each, it was a comparatively easy task. A few men could do it and bolt the sections around the shaft. Conn and the others set to unloading a long trainload of steel which had arrived during the night.

This was the steel for the actual wheel, far lighter and easier to handle than the heavy tower material they had been using. The girders were mostly latticed, strong but comparatively light in weight. There were countless slender steel rods that would form the spokes, the braces, and stays of the wheel. Conn was astonished by the slimness of the spoke rods, and their length. The longest stretched out over four flatcars.

He was a bit dismayed too by the number of them, especially when Uncle Patrick informed the weary crew that this was only the first installment. There would be a new shipment every week until the job was finished.

Two days later the first section of the wheel was hung. Two heavy twenty-one-foot girders which would be part of the outer rim were laid out. To these were bolted two crossbeams, forming a square, hung from its corners by four of the long spoke rods running far up to the hub. At each corner beside the spoke rods were set up four long, thirty-foot girders. The tops of these were connected by four lighter girders which would form part of the inner ring. The result was an open box-like affair hanging from the hub by the four slender spokes. It was braced by lighter rods running crosswise and diagonally. Each rod was fitted with turnbuckles, and when these were tightened the cagelike box was taut, rigid, and tremendously strong.

Mr. Ferris, Uncle Patrick, and Stonewall Jackson stood looking it over.

"Well there we are," Uncle Patrick said dubiously. "One section done. Real handsome and all, but it's took us four days and there's thirty-five more to do. Four times thirty-five's one hundred and forty. One hundred and forty days—four months and twenty days. The fair'll be over."

General Jackson studied his cheroot carefully. "You are unduly pessimistic, Mr. Giblin," he drawled, smiling. "And pessimism has neveh been one of yoah failings. This first section was new to us. With experience we shall easily cut the time to three days foah each. And we shall build two sections simultaneously. You and yoah crew of stalwart Hibernians may take the west half. I and the flowah of the Southland will essay the east. Thus we shall complete two sections every three days. Mr. Ferris's lightning brain will give you the result of that schedule in a moment; it is a trifle beyond my feeble mathematical powers."

"Fifty-two-and-one-half days," Mr. Ferris said promptly, and grinned. "I had figured on sixty days—two months. Anything under sixty belongs to you and your men."

"You are most generous, suh." The General bowed deeply. "We shall look forward with pleasuah to a week or more of leisuah—at full pay."

"But no racing," Mr. Ferris cautioned. "Both sides must proceed at exactly the same rate. The weight must be kept evenly balanced."

"It will, sir, never fear," Uncle Patrick said, greatly relieved. "Three days per section it is. And rest aisy, Stonewall, we'll not keep you and your ragged-tail Rebels waiting, neither."

"Let us trust not," the General smiled. "We shall meet again soon—at the top."

The General was right; with experience the work did go much more rapidly. Each section was merely a repetition of the last; every rod and girder was marked and numbered. The ground crews sent them up in their exact order. Martin Brennan and his crew raised the small derricks, scaffolds, and catwalks each day to keep pace with the rising framework. It became a factory-like routine. The time for the next section was cut to three-and-a-half days, and from then on they averaged three days, sometimes even better.

But it was work, the hardest sort of work. Uncle Patrick drove them unmercifully, doing at least two men's work himself. Conn's every muscle ached, despite the heavy leather gloves his hands were bruised and sore. At night he tossed and tightened bolts in his sleep. No time now for letter writing or for thinking of Wisconsin, or cows.

Luckily the weather favored them with a succession of warm, mild days. Below them the smoothed wastes of soil showed a green fuzz of young grass. The blue waters of Lake Michigan appeared; soon steamers began pushing their way through the scattered ice packs. On the flat farm-lands plowing had started.

They passed the halfway mark, and now the two great arcs of steel began to curve inward toward their eventual meeting. This was the point at which the skeptics had predicted the wheel would collapse. But as each section was added, tightly braced and crossbraced, it became clear that the thirty-foot-deep rim was merely a curved truss bridge, perfectly capable of supporting itself regardless of spokes.

The height at which they now worked was awesome—considerably higher than a twenty-story building. Had he not worked up with it gradually, Conn might have found it terrifying. As it was he gave it no thought; he was too busy.

One day, though, as he and Pop Jenks ate their lunch seated on a crossgirder some two hundred and forty feet above the ground, he remembered with amusement Uncle Patrick's words that first time he had seen him in New

York: "Real men with the heart to do their work at dizzying heights and eat their lunches sitting on a girder no bigger than your two hands with nothing below them but the empty air and maybe a stray sea gull or two."

Well, here he was, doing just that. Uncle Patrick was as good a prophet as Aunt Honora. It must run in the family. Finishing his lunch, he tossed away a scrap of bread and smiled again as a wandering gull from the lake darted through the maze of rods and snatched the morsel in midair.

Each day the tips of the great curving crescent grew closer. Now the rival crews could easily exchange jeers and insults across the narrowing gap. They were cheery insults though, for they had cut their estimated time by a day and a half. At their present rate of progress nine full days of rest, with pay, awaited them.

At last came the day that saw the gap only one section wide. Excitement ran high, for there had been much speculation as to whether the last section would fit. Many had contended that the great unsupported weight would have caused some sag or bending of the two arcs. There had been endless argument and a good number of bets placed. Uncle Patrick had accepted any and all bets. "Mr. Ferris has planned it," he said grandly, "and it will fit as snug as a hard-boiled egg fits its shell."

The last two outer girders would be hoisted up simul-

RL

taneously. Perched on an upper corner of the last section, Conn and Pop Jenks awaited the arrival of their end. On the other side of the wheel sat Uncle Patrick and another worker. Across the twenty-foot gap Stonewall Jackson stood easily on a swaying plank, his hand grasping an upright bar, the smoke from his cheroot rising lazily. Around him his tense crew waited.

Slowly their girder rose. The rival crew caught their end first and pinned it with a bolt or two. Conn, his heart pounding, reached far out, caught his end, and swung it in. The holes lined up almost exactly! Driving his pointed wrench handle through, he levered the holes into perfect alignment: Pop shot through a bolt, spun the nut, and twisted it home with a grunt that was half shout.

At the same instant a roar of triumph from Uncle Patrick announced that his end was fast. Bedlam broke loose as both crews banged their wrenches on rods and girders. The donkeymen tied down their whistles. Mr. Ferris appeared, gazed at the completed circle, waved his hand and returned to his office. Workers on the roofs of nearby buildings waved their hats and cheered. Stonewall Jackson swept off his hat in smiling salute to Uncle Patrick.

Hastily the girders of the inner circle were raised; they fitted perfectly. Both crews united in setting the remaining rods and braces, and by evening the gap was entirely filled.

There was still a week or so of work, stringing more stays, tightening turnbuckles, and removing scaffolding, but it went rapidly.

Came an evening when after gathering up their lunch pails and starting for home, Uncle Patrick, Conn, Martin, and his crew turned for a last look at the great wheel standing still and black against the golden sky.

Every slender rod was taut and trim. The circular sweep of the two rims was clean, and unbroken by derrick or scaffold. The raked legs of the two towers seemed bracing themselves against any gale. Despite the strength and massive weight they knew was there the whole structure gave an impression of lightness and grace.

Uncle Patrick seemed struck with a sudden realization. "By gorry, lad," he roared, clouting Conn a mighty blow on the back, *"our wheel is built!"*

11

Conn and Uncle Patrick did not take off the hard-won nine days. Uncle Patrick was never happy unless working, and Conn was glad to have the extra pay. He was saving his money and now had quite a bit put by. The two Norwegians went as sailors on one of the lake boats. Scrymer set off for San Francisco; later, he said, he might "give Aurstrylier a whirl."

Stonewall and most of the steelworkers departed for other jobs. Conn was sorry to see them go; he had made many warm friends among the daring, happy-go-lucky crew, and his admiration for the General was unbounded. In Conn's gallery of heroes Stonewall Jackson ranked close to Mr. Ferris and Uncle Patrick. To his relief, Martin Brennan decided to stay on. Uncle Patrick could use him for a while.

So busy had they been that they had scarcely noted the actual opening of the Fair some two weeks before. True, on their way to and from work they were aware that the lawns were now beautiful greensward, the shrubbery in full leaf. Where formerly they had picked their way over the frozen hummocks they now trod neatly graveled paths. The lagoons were filled; everywhere elaborate fountains spouted jets and sprays of water; at night, millions of the new electric lights outlined the buildings, flooded the immense courts and plazas with brilliant light. On May first, working high up in the wheel, they had seen the immense antlike throng flowing out of the new railroad station and spreading over the grounds. There had been bands, parades, salutes of cannon. From the Midway now arose a never-ceasing medley of sound—blaring calliopes, the crackle of shooting galleries, German bands, and the raucous bellowing of sideshow barkers.

But for them the wheel *was* the Fair. Until it was completed little else was worthy of notice. Secluded by a high board fence, they went about their work as oblivious of the milling crowds and the activity outside as they had in the windswept days of February.

Next day, as they approached the wheel, Uncle Patrick gave a startled exclamation. "Holy saints and what would this be, a circus or a traveling botanical garden or what? No, by gorry, it's the passenger cars have arrived."

A string of flatcars stood on the siding. On each one stood a long enclosed car gleaming with plate glass, fresh paint, and polished brass. Mr. Ferris and various others were examining them.

"Well, sir, you've done yourself proud," Uncle Patrick cried. "Mr. Pullman's finest palace cars are no more elegant."

They were indeed impressive. Strongly but lightly built on steel frames, the four sides were mostly occupied by windows of heavy plate glass. At either end of each car was a mahogany door fitted with shiny brass hardware. The interiors were commodious, twenty-four feet long by thirteen feet wide—about the size, Conn marveled, of Uncle Michael's living room in New York.

The floors were gay with carpets of green and pink roses on a red background. Down the center stretched two rows of round, tufted plush seats, thirty-eight in all. There were polished brass handrails below the windows, and a monumental brass cuspidor in each corner. A row of glass-shaded electric lights encircled the ceiling. All told, the cars were gay and airy, flooded with light, and would afford a wonderful view.

Hanging the cars to the wheel was simple, and a pleasant change from the driving labor of the actual construc-

1
RL

tion. At either end of each car rose strong hangers which matched holes in the rims of the wheel. As the car was jacked up into position under the wheel, a long steel axle was slid through holes and hangers and bolted fast to the rims, and the job was done, the car free to swing easily as the wheel turned. Their only difficulty was Uncle Patrick's ferocious solicitude for the plate glass and shiny paint. "You'd think we were handling the Vaynus de Meelo herself the way he carries on," Martin Brennan chuckled.

As each car was hung, the wheel was revolved slightly with winch and tackle to receive the next. The driving mechanism was not yet completed, although the engine had arrived and mechanics were busy installing it.

The relaxed pace gave Conn and Martin a little more time to explore the Fair. The evenings were long now, the air pleasant: after dinner, most nights, they would stroll over and look around. The exhibits were interesting, many quite impressive, but before long they always ended up at the German Village or Old Vienna, where Conn eagerly scanned the crowds, looking for a familiar face. The visitors here were mostly Germans, almost all happily eating and drinking.

"There must be all the Germans in America here," said Conn hopelessly.

"And with a scattering from Canada, likely," Martin

agreed. "Lots of blue-eyed lasses with yellow hair, but none would interest you. If there was only a laundry or a washtub, now, it's there we'd be finding her surely, scrubbing somebody or something."

Well the summer is long, Conn reflected, she'll be bound to come sometime. If he couldn't find her at least he could write.

Dear Trudy,

The cars for the wheel have come and we're hanging them. They're that elegant. And *big,* much bigger than I was looking for. One of them would make a nice little house to be living in; I've seen many a cottage in Ireland was smaller. Uncle Patrick says all a fellow would need to make it a home would be a cook stove and a dog and a cat. Martin Brennan says a wife would be handy, too, but Uncle Patrick says it's an unnecessary complication.

Martin Brennan and I go to the German Village and Old Vienna almost every evening looking for you, but we haven't seen you yet. Aren't Germans the great ones for eating?

Your friend,
Conn.

A trainload of lumber arrived, accompanied by a small army of carpenters. Offices, ticket booths, ramps, runways, and waiting rooms sprang up with the overnight suddenness of mushrooms. Broad flights of steps and covered platforms for the passengers grew. The platforms were on three different levels so that six cars could be loaded and unloaded at one time.

Electricians swarmed over the wheel, stringing wires for the lights. Painters were everywhere, gardeners tidied the grounds. Under the wheel itself the mechanics worked steadily on the driving mechanism.

Conn and Martin had often speculated on how this huge weight of steel with its loaded cars would be revolved safely. Now they learned.

In building the wheel they had noticed that the steel plates that formed the outer circumference were cut every two feet by semicircular notches. The reason for these now became clear. The driving mechanism was simply two enormous link chains, similar to mammoth bicycle chains. The cross-links of these chains were steel bars about the size of rolling pins. When the chains were stretched under the wheel these cross-bars fitted exactly into the notches of the rims and thus carried the engine's driving force to the wheel.

Surprisingly enough, the engine, although a beautifully built affair, was quite small, a fact which was explained to them by the elderly engineer. " 'Tis not speed we want," he said with a smile. "To be making the passengers seasick and calling on their Maker. The way it's

geared down, the wheel will be revolving slow and majestic while Little Betsy here whirls away busy as a grandmother's spinning wheel. 'Tis dignity we'll have and power and perfect control, the way the cars'll start and come to rest without the passenger's awareness. It's a beautiful arrangement Mr. Ferris has made for driving that mighty mass of steel and humanity, the work of a genius indeed.'' He went back to polishing the engine's already mirrorlike brasswork.

That evening Conn sat in their room at Mrs. Murphy's writing a letter—to Trudy. Uncle Patrick, his huge frame tilted back in a rocker, eyed his nephew's efforts with an amused smile. Martin Brennan, stretched on his bed, appeared absorbed in a dime novel.

"Conn, lad," Uncle Patrick said finally, "in a week or so I'll be leaving for a new job of Mr. Ferris's, the big cantilever bridge at St. Louis. Are you for it?"

Conn laid down his pencil, his brow wrinkled in thought. He had known that this decision would have to come some time, but he had never really thought it out. He searched for words.

"I don't know, Uncle Patrick," he answered doubtfully. "The work's fine and I'm obligated to you—but I don't know. I don't think I want to be forever moving from one job to another with no home or settled place of my own. It's been a grand experience building the wheel, but now it's built I don't seem to want to go off and leave it. I'm maybe wanting to ride it like Aunt Honora said, 'You'll ride the greatest wheel in all the world.' It's my fortune to ride it, not just to build it, and I don't think I want to be moving on."

"If it's settling down you want you could have done it well in New York," Uncle Patrick said. "You still can. You'll have a fine opportunity with Michael—make bags of money—be his partner some day—and from the way his Agnes looks you over you'll likely be more than a partner."

"She's my cousin," Conn said. "Cousins don't marry."

"Don't they indeed? The royal families of the world do little else and who are you to be setting yourself above dukes and earls and princes?"

"Well I'm no prince and I'm not marrying her. And I'm not slaving my life away building sewers for bags of money to be spending on apartments and dressing up like a dude every night, going to theayters and driving a carriage in the park—"

"You'll be wanting to settle on a farm?" Uncle Patrick asked.

"With cows maybe, and to be making cheeses?" added Martin, grinning.

Conn reddened. "A farm, maybe," he admitted. "But anyway some place of my own, the way you can be driving a nail to hang your overalls on and know that tomorrow and next month and next year the same nail'll be there in the same place."

"It's the Kilroy in you," Uncle Patrick said resignedly. "Your father, God rest his soul, had the love of the land on him and nothing could stir him from his bit cottage and his acre or two of stony ground. I'm one for letting a man choose his own life and good luck to him, and I'll not be influencing anyone to go a path that he can see no happiness in. At the least I've made a man of you, the way you'll not be scratching ditches in the dirty streets of New York and catering to politicians that hand out the jobs, the kind you'd have to be counting the silver every time they came to dinner."

Next morning Uncle Patrick passed by the busy workers at the wheel and led Conn straight to Mr. Ferris's office.

"Mr. Ferris," he said, "my nephew has fallen enamored of your wheel the way he can't bear to be parted from it, even for the St. Louis job. Can you give him work of some sort nursemaiding it?"

"Very easily," Mr. Ferris laughed and looked at Conn. "I thought you were going to be a construction man, Conn," he said. "What's the matter, don't you like it?"

"I like it fine, sir," Conn said. "Only that—"

"Only that he doesn't want to be a migrating tramp like his crazy uncle," Uncle Patrick interrupted. "To always be roaming the country from one job to the next, without kith or kin, or any settled home with a nail to hang his overhauls on."

"Perhaps he's right, at that," Mr. Ferris said, and thought a moment.

"We need guards for the cars," he said. "Thirty-six cars, thirty-six guards. They must be sober, responsible, polite, tactful, and physically fit. We will handle well over a million people in the next four months, and among that many there are bound to be some problems. You will have to deal with timid old ladies, drunks, fussy old gentlemen, an occasional nut, and thousands of children—good, bad, and very bad. Do you think you can handle the job?"

"I can try," Conn said. "I've always got along pretty good with people."

"Fine. Oh yes, and you'll have to wear a uniform. It's pretty fancy, Mrs. Ferris designed it. A sort of combination of policeman, admiral, and lion tamer. Do you mind?"

"No, sir," Conn said with a grin.

"Good." Mr. Ferris wrote a short note and handed it to Conn. "Take this to Sergeant Keogh, late of the Chicago Police Department; he's in charge of the guards. You will have car number one. You helped hang it so it's your due." He turned to Uncle Patrick.

"Well, Pat," he laughed. "You will have to manage that St. Louis job without him. You've lost a good steel man and I've gained a good guard."

12

The wheel was finished, completely finished. The last carpenter and electrician had gone. The painters had departed, leaving booths, ticket offices, and waiting rooms odorous of fresh paint and varnish.

To Conn and Uncle Patrick, looking up at the towering mass, it all seemed unreal, impossible. The setting sun bathed the top of the wheel in golden light, reflected fire from the gleaming windows of the cars, struck sparkles from the shining brass. The lower part was in shadow; the platform where they stood was dim.

Instinctively both their minds went back to that far-off freezing January day when Mr. Ferris had so confidently predicted that the wheel would be operating between the fifteenth and the twentieth of June. This was the evening of June twentieth. Tomorrow the wheel would be turning.

"Did you ever think it would be, Uncle Patrick?" Conn asked. "That it would be done in time—or ever?"

"Mr. Ferris said it would," Uncle Patrick answered with beautiful simplicity.

The last few days had been hectic ones for Conn, as for everyone else. Sergeant Keogh had vigorously trained his guards from sun-up to sundown. Each morning they lined up with military precision for inspection, smart as West Pointers in their handsome new uniforms. White cotton gloves were immaculate, shoes, belts, and buttons highly polished, chins freshly shaven.

There followed strenuous exercises in wrestling, boxing, and the latest methods of subduing unruly customers, should any appear. Unobtrusively tucked in each guard's hip pocket was a short, shot-filled billy which he was taught to use efficiently, and draped across his chest was a nickel chain attached to a police whistle for emergency use.

In addition to all this were lessons in politeness and first aid, and incessant fire drills. Using a large map of the fairgrounds, each guard was required to memorize all the important Fair buildings as well as most of the landmarks of Chicago. "And no matter how much you know," the Sergeant added, "somebody will think up some blithering question you don't. In which case, use your imagination."

* * *

Mr. Ferris joined them and for some time the three contemplated the wheel in silence. "Well, Pat," Mr. Ferris finally said, "we seem to have done it. I promised that it would be in operation by June twentieth and this is June twentieth. I promised that it would be safe and it is safe. However, Mrs. Ferris and I will try it out first, as usual. Tonight. Conn, I would like you to be here—in uniform. Mrs. Ferris hasn't yet seen her creation and I know she would like to. You set it off well. It may be rather late; we have a dinner engagement."

He shook hands warmly with Uncle Patrick. "Pat," he said, "I can't begin to tell you how much I owe you. Once more you have made a dream come true. Without you I might have a brain of sorts, but no hands. Thank you for all you've done."

That evening Conn in all his glory waited on the empty platform. For the first time the cars were lighted, making the huge wheel the most conspicuous feature of the entire fairgrounds.

The boiler had been fired up and now sizzled quietly; the Negro fireman dozed. Mr. Barry, the elderly engineer, ceased his everlasting polishing and wandered over to chat with Conn. "Little Betsy's just raring to go," he said. "I'd just as lief they'd come along soon so we could give that old wheel a spin. Everything ready and she hasn't made a full revolution yet. Oh well, she'll make plenty tomorrow, I'm thinking, with all the world clamoring for a ride on her.'' He wandered back, looked at his gauges, screwed down a grease cup or two, and settled in a chair with a copy of *Nick Carter*.

For the hundredth time Conn went over his instructions—*When the car comes to rest you will unlock the north door and say, ''All out please. Those wishing another ride will please purchase tickets at the ticket booth.'' When all passengers are out you will re-lock the north door and unlock and open the south door. You will then say, ''All aboard please. Kindly step to the far end of the car.'' When all passengers are aboard you will close and lock the south door. Remember:* **BOTH DOORS MUST ALWAYS BE LOCKED AND THE KEY IN YOUR POCKET EXCEPT WHEN LOADING AND UNLOADING.**

Conn went through the routine of locking and unlocking the doors and putting the key in his pocket a half dozen times. He was so busy with it that he failed to notice the Ferrises' arrival until he heard their voices. They both wore evening clothes, and Conn thought Mrs. Ferris was the most beautiful vision he had ever beheld.

''You must be Conn,'' she said, offering a hand, ''Mr. Giblin's nephew. Mr. Ferris has spoken of you often.'' She stepped back and inspected him carefully. ''The uniform is quite effective, if I do say so,'' she laughed. ''And *most* becoming.'' Conn blushed heavily, adding in his mind that she was also the most gracious person he had ever encountered.

"And aren't the cars beautiful?" Mrs. Ferris went on, stepping into Number One. "So cozy and *so* immaculate. Why one could easily keep house here."

"Uncle Patrick says that all it needs is a cook stove and a dog and a cat to make it a home," Conn ventured.

"And a wife, of course," she laughed. "Haven't you *any* of those things, Conn?"

"No'm," Conn admitted, blushing still more deeply. "I could start with a cat though, easy. Our landlady has eighteen of them."

"No," she said, "that would never do. The wife first, then the cook stove. The cat and dog will come of their own accord."

"If she's a good cook," Conn said with a grin.

Mr. Ferris called them over and handed his wife down the steps to the engine room. He pointed to a few blocks of wood that he had piled on a chair just below the rim of the great wheel. The topmost block was within a half-inch of the curving steel.

"Just a little test for my own satisfaction," he explained. "As you know many of my fellow engineers have said that we could never build a wheel of this size that would be a perfect circle. It would have bulges, they said, it would sag, it would be lopsided. So—it would never

RL

mesh properly with the driving mechanism, it would miss a cog, go out of control and we would have a frightful catastrophe. Now let's see. All right, Mr. Barry, you may proceed."

Mr. Barry gently moved the throttle and Little Betsy went smoothly into eager action. Silently the long driving shaft and its sprocket wheels began to turn; the cross links clanked slightly as they meshed accurately with the notches of the rim. So gently that at first the movement was hardly discernible, the great wheel began to move.

Mr. Barry opened his throttle wide and Little Betsy willingly responded. Now the spinning crankshaft was a blur, the shining steel balls of the governor became a glimmering halo. The clanking of the chain links stepped up its rhythm. The great wheel was moving at its ordained top speed, the rim flashed past their fascinated gaze evenly. The tiny space between steel rim and wooden blocks never varied in the slightest. The wheel could not have been a more perfect circle. Conn drew a great sighing breath of relief as Mr. Barry announced, "Car Number One just passed, she's made a full turn."

"Very good," Mr. Ferris said placidly, "I am quite satisfied. I just wish some of the prophets of disaster could have been here to see that. Give her another turn for good measure, then we'll have our ride." He escorted

Mrs. Ferris up the steps to await the arrival of Conn's car.

"I'm thinking if anyone told Uncle Patrick that test ought to be made he'd have knocked his teeth out," Conn observed.

"I am sure he would have, bless him," Mrs. Ferris laughed. "His faith in Mr. Ferris's calculations is almost alarming at times, but inspiring too."

Mr. Barry brought the wheel to such a smooth, gentle stop that the cars scarcely swayed. Conn sprang to open the door of Number One and his passengers stepped aboard.

"All right, Conn, do your duty and lock us in," Mr. Ferris said. "Tell Barry to give us a full turn and then stop when we're at the top. We'd like to admire the view. I'll switch off the lights so we can see better. When they go on you can bring us down."

Conn locked the door and stepped back, Mrs. Ferris smiled and waved, Mr. Barry opened the throttle, and the great Ferris Wheel began it first trip carrying passengers.

Conn was amazed at the soundlessness of it. There was something eerie in the sight of this great mass of steel, more than two million pounds of it, rising, turning, and descending, steadily, smoothly, all without any sound save for the slight clanking of the roller chains on their sprockets. One would have expected creaks and groans, squeals and scrapings and rattles, but there were none. It was so still that the sudden clang of the boiler door shutting rang with startling loudness.

Car One passed and rose again. When it reached the summit, Mr. Barry brought the wheel to a gentle stop. He resumed his perusal of *Nick Carter* and the fireman again dozed. The bright windows of Car Number One became black.

It was late now; all over the fairgrounds the lights were going out. The sounds of the Midway faded away. From the lagoons, where thousands of frogs had accepted the new ordering of their world, rose a steady chorus. A midnight mist was rising.

A group of Negroes—Pullman porters, perhaps, from the railroad station, or waiters from one of the restaurants—were making their way homeward, out beyond the wheel. They were singing an old spiritual and there was one tenor voice that rose through the darkness sweet and soaring as the flight of a gull. There was a full strong baritone that came and went, now losing itself in the organ-like chords of the basses, now rising lone and free, tossing out the words clear and stirring as a trumpet call:

> Ezekiel saw the wheel
> Way up in the middle of the air,

Ezekiel saw the wheel
Way in the middle of the air.
And the little wheel ran by faith
And the big wheel ran by the grace of God,
It's a wheel in a wheel
Way in the middle of the air.

The Midway was almost silent now. Somewhere a dog barked and from the lake came the long hoot of a steamer whistle. The last train pulled out of the railroad station, its bell clanging. "Ezekiel saw the wheel," sang the tenor voice, "Way up in the middle of the air . . ."

The mist became thicker, rising halfway up the glowing circle of lighted cars. It blotted out the buildings and the towers so that the great ring seemed to float in the air without earthly ties. Mr. Barry put down his *Nick Carter*. The singers were drifting into the distance, but the voices, though fainter, still rang hauntingly clear and moving:

And the little wheel ran by faith
And the big wheel ran by the grace of God,
It's a wheel in a wheel
Way—in the—middle—of—the—air.

After a few long moments the lights flashed on and the car descended. Mrs. Ferris stepped out, her eyes suspiciously moist.

"Wasn't it beautiful, Conn?" she cried. "The singing. Did you hear it? 'The little wheel ran by faith and the big wheel ran by the grace of God.' "

"It's a sign, surely ma'am," Conn said.

"It is, I am sure," she agreed. "And we *were* way up in the middle of the air. The mist hid everything below, but the stars were clear and bright and all around us. I think it has been the most wonderful evening of my life."

Mr. Ferris, looking supremely happy, cleared his throat. "Thank you for coming, Conn," he said. "It has been a great experience; I hope others find it as thrilling. It was fun having our wheel all to ourselves, but what was it Louis the something said, 'After me, the deluge?' After us, the multitude—of cash customers—we hope. Better get a good sleep, tomorrow you'll have a busy day."

As Conn walked home through the misty darkness the haunting spiritual still ran through his head. "The little wheel ran by faith . . ." It seemed to give him a word and a meaning that had been eluding him.

What was it that had rung so unquestioningly in Uncle Patrick's simple answer this afternoon when he declared, "Mr. Ferris said it would"? What had suddenly moved Martin Brennan and Scrymer to nonchalantly ride the great shaft, rising on its untried tackle? Why did Stonewall Jackson's men daily risk their lives at the mere wave of his walking stick? No one had ever ridden the great wheel before, but Mrs. Ferris's only thought had been for the beauty of it all. What was it that had shone so steadily in Trudy's eyes that last evening on the ship as she said with such serene certainty, "I will wait and you will come, it is your fortune"?

He had been unable to put a name to it, but now he knew. Softly he hummed the song that he would never forget:

> And the little wheel ran by faith
> And the big wheel ran by the grace of God,
> It's a wheel in a wheel
> Way in the middle of the air.

13

Mr. Ferris was right—the next day was a busy one. The morning was given over to a reception and free ride for the city and Fair officials, the men who had supplied the financial backing, prominent engineers and scientists, and everyone else of importance—all, of course, with their families. Uncle Patrick, unfamiliar in his Sunday garb, wandered about in the crowd for a while, but before long found more congenial company in the engine room with Mr. Barry. They were soon joined by Martin Brennan.

The guards stood rigidly at attention by their cars. Conn, looking over the throng, could identify only one familiar face, that of Mr. Zillheimer. The pork packer was accompanied by his wife, their three sons, and their wives and children. All the sons and all their children were large, pink, and scrubbed-looking, all remarkably alike in appearance. They all look like Zillheimer Products, Conn thought.

The six lower cars were open for inspection, and the entire Zillheimer family wandered into Number One, solemnly inspecting its appointments. The pork magnate confronted Conn. "I've seen you before," he announced.

"In Ferris's office. The day I decided to put some money into this."

Conn, who was not aware that Mr. Zillheimer had even glanced in his direction on that occasion, agreed. "Yes, sir," he said. "That was my first day on the job."

"You worked on the wheel?"

"Yes, sir," Conn answered with some pride. "From the bottom of the foundation holes to the last girder on the top of it."

"Good job," Mr. Zillheimer said. He looked up at the immense network of interlacing rods and girders. "Well built.'' He went into the car and settled himself solidly on one of the round seats. Two of the youngest grandchildren climbed into his lap and went to sleep.

Mrs. Ferris suddenly appeared. She smiled at the placid domestic scene. ''Well, Mr. Zillheimer,'' she called gaily, ''you seem to trust our wheel completely.''

''Sure,'' the packer said with a smile. ''I don't put money in anything I can't trust; I don't put my family in it either.''

Mrs. Ferris smiled at Conn and touched his arm. *''And the little wheel ran by faith,''* she hummed softly.

One or two aldermen and their wives joined the Zillheimers in Number One; the other five cars filled up. Mr. Barry gave a long blast of the whistle, the guards closed and locked their doors, and the trip began.

This was Conn's first ride as a passenger and he was surprised by the gentle, soundless movement. Before anyone was fully aware that the car was in motion they were floating quietly up above the surrounding buildings. When they were two-thirds the height of the towers, there was a few moments' pause as the next six cars were loaded. On the third pause they were at the summit, and even Mr. Zillheimer rose and strode to the window to admire the view. The whole family lost its porklike stolidity as the great sweep of the fairgrounds, the city, and the lake unfolded itself before them.

"There's the plant, Pop," exclaimed the oldest son excitedly. "And there's Lake Shore Drive. There's our house too—see?—with the trees and the pointed roofs."

His father grunted agreement. "And there's the stock-yards," he added. "So clear you can almost smell 'em."

The sixth stop brought them down just above the now almost empty loading platforms. Great as the throng had been, the huge wheel had swallowed it up easily; most of the cars were only partly filled. It was noticeable, however, that quite a number of the invited guests had quietly withdrawn, and were standing in small groups, timorously watching the turning wheel.

"Quitters," snorted Mr. Zillheimer contemptuously. "Glad to take the profits, but scared to risk their own precious hides. Look at old Peabody there, waiting to see if his meal ticket's going to get killed. Phooie!" He made a derisive gesture as the car passed, to which Mr. Peabody responded with a sickly grin.

After the last pause the car made one slow, stately revolution, then began unloading. Conn unlocked the north door and automatically recited, "All out please. Those wishing another ride will please purchase tickets at the ticket booth."

"Sure," Mr. Zillheimer laughed contentedly, "I'll take plenty more. Once a week, anyway."

At noon the gates were opened to the public, and once

more Mr. Ferris's calculations were proven correct: thousands were clamoring to ride the great wheel. Long lines of eager customers passed by the ticket booths, and the turnstiles clicked busily. The platforms became packed with people. Every car was filled to its legal limit of sixty persons, yet the completion of each trip found still larger crowds awaiting their turn.

And the people loved it. As each car rose higher and higher they crowded to the windows, exclaiming over the vastness of the panorama spread before them, gasping at the height, recognizing landmarks with excited cries. True, a few became dizzy or frightened, some children wept, but the smooth, steady movement and the obvious strength and solidity of the huge wheel soon reassured even the most timid.

At six o'clock there was a welcome half-hour's halt that enabled the weary attendants to eat their supper; then the gates were reopened and the crowds swarmed in, in even greater numbers. The last trip, ending at midnight, found Conn almost as weary as any of the hectic construction days.

As he sleepily started homeward, he was joined by Martin Brennan. Martin revealed that he had accepted a job in the German Village for the summer. Not that he needed it especially, he had quite a bit laid by; it was more in the nature of a vacation—with pay.

"It is simple and easy," the little man said, "I just sit on a comfortable stool and rake in the cash. They're a kindly, clean people and it's a real pleasure to be watching how they enjoy their beer and food. From my perch I have a fine view of all who come and go, the way I might just be seeing your young lady from Wisconsin and directing her to Car Number One of the great Ferris Wheel."

"She'll come," Conn said confidently. "She'll come and ride the wheel before the summer's gone."

Uncle Patrick left for the St. Louis job, and Conn soon settled into the regular routine. For the first few days the crowds were tremendous, then they leveled off to a regular steady flow. On weekdays the cars were always comfortably filled; on Saturdays and Sundays they were jammed to capacity.

Weekday mornings were the least crowded, and Conn was surprised to find that he had several regular passengers. There was an elderly gentleman who appeared at the door of Car Number One every Monday morning on the dot of nine. Immediately the door was opened he strode briskly to the end seat nearest the north door, sat down, and began to read his morning paper. As the car reached the halfway mark in its ascent he folded his paper, stood at the door, and stared fixedly out at the panorama of city and lake. Then as the descending car reached the level of the tower tops he sat down again and continued his reading. At the end of the trip he nodded curtly to Conn and went on his way. Conn never knew who he was or anything about him, but the man never skipped a Monday morning the entire summer.

There was an artist who rode all morning every day for three weeks. He was making a drawing of the outspread fairgrounds. Conn, looking over his shoulder, didn't think much of the drawing. He wondered why the man didn't take a picture of the view with one of those new-fangled Kodaks that were becoming so popular, but he didn't like to ask.

And there was a tiny little old lady who came every Tuesday morning just before lunch. She carried a small mesh shopping bag from which she always extracted a neatly wrapped sandwich, a small pair of opera glasses, and a notebook. After eating the sandwich she would adjust the opera glasses and peer out at the birds, pausing occasionally to write something in the notebook. There weren't many birds around as far as Conn had noticed; a few pigeons had taken to roosting on the towers, the fairgrounds swarmed with sparrows, now and then a gull soared past, but the little old lady seemed to discover much of interest. Each Tuesday as she left the car she would fix Conn with her nearsighted eyes and state,

"Great and wonderous are the ways of nature." There was no denying that, so Conn would nod agreement and she would pick her way off through the crowd.

There were several others who returned again and again, fascinated by the thrilling ride and the wide view. Among them none was more enthusiastic than Mr. Zillheimer. He arrived at least once a week, shepherding a party of friends, relatives, or customers. He always picked Conn's car, usually chatted with him a bit, and at the conclusion of the trip always unobtrusively forced a dollar bill on him. Conn didn't like to accept it, but he didn't like to seem rude by refusing it either, Mr. Zillheimer was so pleasant and friendly. In one of his letters to Trudy, Conn wrote, "I am saving all the dollar bills Mr. Zillheimer gives me. Maybe when I settle down somewhere I'll be buying a pig with the money. I could give it the namc of Zilly."

Now that the work was more regular and not too tiring, Conn found more time for writing. The unmailed letters in his bureau drawer had grown to be quite a packet. Uncle Patrick's and Mrs. Ferris's comments on the possibilities of housekeeping in Car Number One had set him to dreaming of it in some detail. Often, when the demands of the passengers allowed, he planned likely arrangements.

The two rows of seats of course would have to go. A

front and a back door too, for such a small house, hardly seemed necessary. And if he put the stove at the south end as he planned, it might be in the way of the door. On the other hand a door there would be very convenient for bringing in the stove wood without tramping through the parlor. Of course the stove could go halfway down the car, against the back wall, but that would divide the space rather awkwardly.

Then there was the problem of windows. It was nice to have that many windows; it made things light and cheery and one could see out in every direction. But it might make things very hot in the summer and would probably fade the carpet. He'd better ask Trudy's advice.

". . . A fellow could be building out a little roof on the sunny side," he wrote, "a porch like. It would be a pleasant place for the dog and the cat to lie or to sit of an evening, and a good spot for sunning the milk pails. But where to put the stove has me clean bewildered. . . .

"I would divide off the sleeping room with a curtain that could be pulled across and have a bed the like of a ship's bunk, built solid against the wall, the way in the daytime it wouldn't look like a bedroom at all. Of course it wouldn't be stylish like the brass beds Uncle Michael has in his flat, but they're clumsy things and make me think of the monkey cage in the zoo. . . ."

There came a day of thunderstorms and pouring rain.

Customers were few, and those who did brave the rain were terrified of the lightning, although assured that the great steel wheel, well grounded in the earth, was the safest place they could find.

The lashing rain streaming down the windows made the car cozier than ever and gave Conn several more ideas. That night he wrote, "I'll have to be building little porches at the two doors to keep out the rain when the doors are opened and for a place to be wiping the mud off my boots. . . .

". . . And I'll be building little gutters on the eaves of the roof to run the water into a rain barrel. My mother was always saying there's nothing like good soft rain-water, just what for I disremember, but anyway a rain-barrel is a handy place to put fish in you'd be catching in a pond or a stream and keeping alive in a bucket. The way they'll stay swimming and fresh for days and be right there for cooking when you'd want them. I'm told there's no gamekeepers here in America and you can be catching the fish in any pond or stream you've a mind to. . . ."

In his mind and in his letters Conn gradually built up his dream. The view—there would be no ocean or Kilda Point, but there would be water of some kind, a pond or even a lake—perhaps Lake Michigan. The flowers around the house, climbing over the porches. The vegetable garden—with no potato blight. A small barn for the cow.

"I've enough saved for a cow now," he wrote. "Only one at first, but maybe more later. We could be selling the cream to your Uncle Otto maybe for his cheese making. . . ."

Conn suddenly laid down his pencil, a bit aghast. "*We,*" he had written. "*We could be selling the cream.*"

Of course he had vaguely realized that all this dream really had been built around "We"—around himself and Trudy, but this was the first time he had used the actual word or even fully admitted it to himself. It had always been "I could," or "a fellow could." This might be going a bit too far, taking too much for granted. Trudy doubtless had ideas of her own. She might already be married to some blond, husky young German.

Then he laughed at himself. The whole thing was only a dream anyway. It was largely built around Car Number One, and Car Number One was an integral part of a huge steel construction, a million-dollar enterprise, the great Ferris Wheel. Besides, in all likelihood the letters never would be mailed. Realizing that, he could write and dream more freely.

". . . I remember now what it was my mother was always saying about rain water; that it was fine for washing anyone's hair. I'm thinking that after you've washed your hair and it drying in the sun, it would be the like of a golden waterfall flowing down your back. My mother said the rainwater was good for the complexion too, but you'd not be needing that at all."

The next day Uncle Michael and his family arrived from New York.

14

Standing by the door of Car Number One, ready for the first trip of the day, Conn suddenly found himself engulfed in family. Agnes's arms were around his neck, Aunt Cecilia was shaking his hands, Uncle Michael, shouting greetings, was pounding his back. As the other guards looked on in amusement Conn, blushing furiously, disengaged himself, straightened his cap and announced, "All aboard please. Kindly step to the far end of the car."

The car was fairly full, the passengers crowded to the windows, but the family clustered around Conn, bombarding him with questions. When he was coming back to New York? Had he really worked high up on this terrifying wheel? Why hadn't he written oftener? How was Uncle Patrick?

Conn answered them all rather vaguely. The others went to look out and he was left alone with Agnes. Agnes was not interested in the view.

"But Conn dear, you *will* be coming back to New York as soon as this silly Fair is over?" she asked.

"I don't think so."

"But Conn, what will you do?"

"I don't know—"

"To think of you being dressed up in this silly uniform, like a doorman or something. It's so *menial*. Papa is dying to have you back in the company. He's making just loads of money."

"I've got a good job here," Conn answered. "I don't mind the uniform." He was not going to be "worked on" like Uncle Michael.

"But only until the Fair ends. Then they'll tear down your precious wheel. Then what?"

"I don't know," Conn said desperately. "Why don't you look at the view, Agnes? People come from all over the country to look at it."

"I didn't come to look at any old view, Conn. You will have dinner with us tonight won't you? We're staying at the Congress Hotel."

"I have to work, we work till midnight. Besides I haven't any dude clothes." Conn didn't think it necessary to explain that there were alternate guards so scheduled that each attendant had one free day a week.

Agnes switched away and joined the others. She pretended a lively interest in the view, but Conn could see that it was not very genuine. When the trip was over the family again gathered around.

"Wish you had some time off, lad," Uncle Michael said. "Tomorrow's New York Day and there'll be a lot of important people here. Like to have you meet them. We'll have to be doing a bit of entertaining, some big contracts hanging fire."

Conn grinned, remembering Uncle Patrick's words, ". . . catering to politicians . . . the kind you'd have to be counting the silver every time they come to dinner."

"Tommy Glynn's coming tomorrow too," Agnes said. "He found it hard to get away because Papa depends on him so much. He's very important in the company now. He's coming on the Exposition Flyer with Alderman Crawley. He sent me a telegram last night."

"Good for Tommy," Conn said with some relief. "He's a hard worker. Tell him to come and ride the wheel."

"Oh, Tommy can't be bothering with silly things like that," Agnes tossed her head. "He has really important matters to attend to."

They departed, and Conn resumed his duties. There

was a more carefree lilt than usual to his voice as he called, "All aboard, please. Kindly step to the far end of the car."

Agnes appeared once more on Saturday afternoon, clinging to the arm of a proud and elaborately garbed Tommy Glynn. Conn greeted them warmly; he had always liked Tommy—he was serious minded, hardworking, and decent. Not too bright, perhaps, but he'd get along. Tommy didn't realize that he was being worked on, but he wouldn't have minded much if he had. He was a good-natured lad and he would be a partner one day. Agnes would see to that.

Conn's car was full, so they had to take Number Two. After the ride they stopped to tell him good-by; the family was leaving that night. Conn shook Tommy's hand warmly. "Good-by, Tommy," he said. "You're doing fine. Good luck to you—in everything." Tommy reddened and grinned.

Agnes kissed him good-by. "See what you've driven me to," she whispered, "you stubborn brute." Then she bit his ear—sharply—but she was smiling her old impish smile and didn't look too heartbroken.

She'll do fine, Conn thought, after they had gone; Tommy's good material to work on. She'll have her apartment and her carriage and a lot of elegant silver—to be counting after their friends leave.

That night he wrote:

Dear Trudy,

My Uncle and Aunt and Cousins were here and have gone now. They wanted me to come back to New York and build sewers, but I've no mind to do it. It's no place there for a cow or a dog or a cat, only goats you'll see climbing the craggy rocks among the shanties uptown. And I'd rather be walking the dust of a country road with no shoes at all than be riding a carriage in Central Park with my feet crying their torture buttoned in patent-leather boots, and a collar to my neck so tall it would be choking the breath out of an ostrich. . . .

I'm thinking the cook stove would be best at the end after all, but a little away from the corner. The wood-box could go in the corner and that would leave room for the door to swing open. . . . There are elegant shrubs and flowers here on the grounds. A rose called Dorothy Perkins would be pretty climbing over the porch.

There is a Livestock Palace too with horses and cattle and swine and sheep would make you dizzy there's so many. Martin Brennan and I go there on our day off. Being on the sea all his life he hardly knows a horse from a sheep, but like all sailors he thinks he knows the world and all about them. He saw some cows in Germany once called Holsteins he says are best, but I've more liking for the Jerseys. They're so small and gentle, but I don't know would they thrive in Wisconsin. . . .

The summer drifted along uneventfully—hot July and hotter August. On especially warm nights the wheel was always crowded to capacity with sweltering people seeking the cooler breezes of the upper air. Conn had no unpleasant experiences, although some of the other guards had a few. Tom Sheridan of Car Number Six drew a maniac who was bent on trying to commit suicide by jumping out a window, but was quickly subdued with the aid of Tom's billy. Sometimes of a Saturday evening a whistle would sound from one of the cars, the wheel would turn, and a few over-stimulated carousers would be ejected and turned over to the Columbian Guards.

Conn got along well with people, on the whole. The only ones who irritated him were those who messed up his car; with such as dropped gum on the carpet or smeared the windows with sticky hands he was quite sharp, for he took great pride in Number One's appearance. Its windows were always the cleanest, its brass and woodwork always the most highly polished of all the thirty-six. It was always Car Number One that Mr. and Mrs. Ferris selected for unusually distinguished guests; Mr. Zillheimer, on his frequent visits, would use no other.

September came, and the fields of the outspread farms were being harvested. Great threshing machines sent up towering clouds of black smoke, dust and chaff floated in golden drifts, the woodlots burst into flaming squares of red and orange, the cattle were turned out to graze in the mowed fields. The moon rose fat and golden like a rich cheese. Wisconsin Day came, with thousands of flaxen-haired Germans. It went—and still no Trudy.

There arrived an announcement of the forthcoming marriage of Miss Agnes Theresa Giblin to Mr. Thomas Aloysius Glynn. Conn wrote, wishing her great happiness.

October came in with nightly frosts. The woodlots were becoming a uniform brown. Conn could see men packing leaves around the foundations of the farmhouses, putting up storm-windows, stacking great ranks of cordwood. The Fair crowds were thinning out, although the wheel still did a good business.

As the days hastened by at a frightening speed, Conn's hopes began to waver. The stack of letters had grown so large that he had to tie it with a bit of string. On October fifteenth he wrote:

> Today is the fifteenth and the Fair closes on the twenty-sixth—only eleven more days and you haven't come yet. If you don't come at all I don't know what I'll do. Go to Wisconsin and look for you I guess, though they say it's a big state and it might take years to find you. I still have faith you'll come, but you'd better hurry.
>
> Martin Brennan has a friend at the German Village comes from Wisconsin—from Milwaukee. She's a widow lady

would make two of him for size, but very kind and pleasant-spoken. She doesn't mind at all the small size of him or his crookedness. Maybe she'll marry him, but I don't know. He says it wouldn't be right to be wishing his crippled carcass on a fine healthy young woman the like of her, but I tell him he's only proud and stubborn. . . .

The nice carpet of the car isn't as bright colored as it was, but it's only that it needs a good cleaning. . . .

Tonight was a new moon so thin it looked like a nail paring. . . .

The next morning, the sixteenth, Mr. Ferris strolled up to chat with Conn.

"Well, Conn," he said. "Only ten more days and you'll be a free man. What are you planning to do with your freedom?"

"I don't know at all, Mr. Ferris," Conn answered. "I've not settled in my mind. I'll find a job, I suppose."

"Without the slightest trouble," Mr. Ferris said with a smile. "Your Uncle Patrick wants you on the St. Louis job, or I'd like you with me, if you'd care for office work. And Zillheimer has taken a great fancy to you; I'm sure he'll be making you an offer—that is, if you're interested in pork."

"Only for the eating," Conn laughed. "I don't know, Mr. Ferris," he went on. "Maybe I'll look around a bit.

I hadn't much thought about what to do, once the wheel's gone."

Mr. Ferris gazed up at the great mass of steel. "The wheel has been quite an event in your life, hasn't it, Conn?" he said. "It has in mine too. You and I are about the only ones here who have been with it from first to last. It will be a rather sad day when the wreckers move in. I'm planning to be in St. Louis then; I wouldn't want to see it come down."

Conn rubbed the shiny brass key of Number One on his sleeve. "Me neither," he said. "It'll be a sorry day the last time I lock the doors of Number One. But it's been a great and wonderful thing, Mr. Ferris—nothing like it ever before."

Mr. Ferris nodded understandingly, and started away, then stopped. "Speaking of Zillheimer," he said, "there he is now, for his usual weekly ride."

The pork magnate advanced, escorting a party of fashionably dressed friends. He greeted Mr. Ferris expansively. "Well, Ferris," he cried, "only ten days left to enjoy our wheel. Got to make the most of it. Like you to meet these folks. This is my brother Otto, from Wisconsin. The only Zillheimer bachelor that ever lived. You know his cheeses—Zillheimer Cheese?"

"Who doesn't?" Mr. Ferris laughed, shaking hands

with the tall, dignified old gentleman. "Eaten Most from Coast to Coast."

At the words "Otto," "Wisconsin," and "cheese," Conn's breath caught short. He was like a steelworker on a high girder suddenly stricken with the fear. He tried desperately to get a good look at the rest of the party, but he couldn't see them well, although there seemed to be something vaguely familiar.

"And my youngest brother Karl," Mr. Zillheimer went on, "just come over from Germany a few months ago. It took us a long time to persuade Karl to leave the old country, but he's a good American now, Otto's right-hand man. This is his wife, Mrs. Karl—and their daughter Trudy. . . ."

But Trudy was not listening, or hearing. Her blue eyes were wide—her hands outstretched. "Conn!" she breathed, stepping eagerly foward. "You have come. I knew you would."

Conn, flushing scarlet, found himself clasping both her hands—stammering confusedly.

"Yes—I came—" he floundered. "Quite a while ago—and—you came—but who—what?"

"Karl, Karl," her mother called excitedly, "it is the nice young man from the boat. You remember? The *City of Bristol*?"

Her father rushed over, beaming. "Of course, of course. The fine young man. You must pardon us we did not know you—the uniform. Otto, meet our fine young friend."

Uncle Otto greeted him warmly. The pork magnate and Mr. Ferris made appropriate, though puzzled, sounds of pleasure. Conn, now completely bewildered, managed to fling open the door of Number One and intone, "All aboard please. Kindly step to the far end of the car."

They all obediently did, but Trudy clung to Conn's arm as he locked the door, her eyes searching his face. "You followed the star and you came," she murmured. "It was your fortune."

"But you?" he said. "Why—in the steerage? You—with millionaire uncles and your grand clothes, letting on like you were common people—like me and Martin Brennan—" His voice was resentful. "Going to milk cows—you! Making me think I could ever—"

"It was father," she interrupted. "He is so proud. Never would he take money from them. Work yes, with Oncle Otto, but never money. So, we came as we could afford—in the steerage—like immigrants. We *were* immigrants—I am proud we were. Many, many fine Americans have come in the steerage—I am glad we did—if we had not I would not have found you."

"A fine lot you found," Conn said bitterly. "*I'm* still an immigrant, working for wages. Dressed up in a flunkey's uniform—"

She smiled contentedly, twisting a polished brass button on his sleeve. "I love your uniform. It is beautiful—but the hat I do not like. It covers up your hair, your fine curling copper hair." Her look became more serious. "But Conn, in America everyone works. My father works—Oncle Otto works, so hard—Uncle Herman works hardest of all. You are no different—I am no different. I am just the same as always."

"No." Conn's mouth was a tight straight line, his flush had faded, his face was a little drawn. "No. You're a real lady now. It's all different."

She studied him silently a moment. A smile was working at her mouth, but her eyes were serious and determined, the blue darker. "I *am* the same," she said slowly. "You will see." She turned away and joined the others.

Conn stood rigidly by the door, but his eyes took in every detail of his passengers. No wonder he had not recognized Trudy. The flaxen hair was now arranged in a pompadour that cast her face into a deep shadow from which her eyes shone with an almost startling blueness. Her hat was of deep-blue velvet ornamented with tiny ribbon bows and sweeping ostrich plumes. A tall collar of fine lace encircled her throat. Her long skirt swept the floor, making her seem unwontedly tall.

It was all very beautiful and expensive and the height of fashion—but it wasn't Trudy. Even her speech was different, more sure, the accent less pronounced, though still fascinating. Only the blue eyes and the Dresden-doll complexion were the same, but they were almost lost in the elaboration of silk and velvet.

His mind was a tumult of emotions; the trip seemed endless, the stops unusually long. It was the greatest relief when he could finally unlock the north door, fling it open and blurt, "All out, please. Those wishing another ride will kindly purchase tickets at the ticket office."

The others passed out, chatting excitedly over the wonders of the ride, but Trudy lingered a moment. Her expression was almost as determined as Conn's now, but the smile still twitched at her lips. "I *am* the same," she said, with a slight toss of the head. "You will see."

That night, propped up in bed, Martin Brennan watched with sympathy and some amusement as Conn paced the floor of their room.

"And aren't I the world's greatest fool," Conn raged.

"Me taking her to be ordinary people like us and her a Zillheimer? Zillheimer's Pork Products—Zillheimer's Cheese—et the most from coast to coast! Uncles the like of Croesus with their millions and me conductor of a skyscraping streetcar. To be writing and dreaming of a one-room shanty and where to put the cook stove and her living in a mansion, likely, with a swarm of servants to do her bidding." He snatched the stack of letters from the bureau drawer and threw it on the table.

Martin Brennan reached out for his pipe, lit it, and puffed placidly. "Whisht, lad," he counseled, "ease off your mainsheet before you'd be bursting a blood vessel or two. The lass is a fine lass, and fine people don't change, only for the better."

"Don't change? And her got up as elegant as Lillian Russell with the fine gold hair of hers pushed out in a pompadour like the roof of a piazza? White kid gloves on her hands and a diamond pin to her throat all the Kilroys in Ireland couldn't buy her with seven years of their pay."

"It's only window dressing, that," Martin said placatingly, "the latest fashions. Would you have her coming to the Fair barefooted and with a shawl on her head? But the heart of her's the same. Listen, you wrong-headed young peat-digger. They came to the Village after they'd rode your wheel and she knew me at once. She come and hung over the counter talking to me as wistful as I'd been selling penny candies and her without the penny to buy them—''

''I'm no penny candy,'' Conn snapped. ''And nobody's buying me.''

'' 'I've seen him, Martin,' she sez, 'and he's changed. He was so stern and cold. In his uniform he was like a Prussian officer in the old country. I was frightened, Martin,' sez she, and the blue eyes of her had tears in them.''

Conn picked up the packet of letters, turned it over once or twice, then flung it in the wastebasket.

''Me boasting I'd saved enough to buy a cow,'' he laughed bitterly. ''One cow—and her precious Uncle Otto with herds of cows would stock a ranch in Texas. I'll be beholden to nobody, Martin. Come next week and the wheel makes its last turn I'll be leaving for St. Louis and the bridge job with Uncle Patrick.''

''You're young, lad, and peacock-proud,'' Martin sighed, knocking out his pipe. ''But I never thought to see you afraid. To think of you working on the dizzy heights of the wheel without a thought beyond your lunch and now frighted as a bewildered chicken by someone else's money. And get this through your concrete skull; you needn't be fretting yourself about being beholden to anybody. I've heard all about your prospective in-laws, and anybody that's born or married into the Zillheimer tribe *works* for his keep. Those three fat sons of the pork man work harder than the lowest-paid laborer in the plant. And Uncle Otto, I'm told, is up at five and out in the barns pitching and bedamming with the best of them for all his seventy years."

"I'll stand on my own two feet," Conn said.

"And tread corns on them for all of me," Martin concluded, pulling up the blanket and turning to the wall. "And I might add that you're a stubborn, pride-blind, contrary-minded mick that only a lady mule-skinner would have the foolishness to think of afflicting herself with."

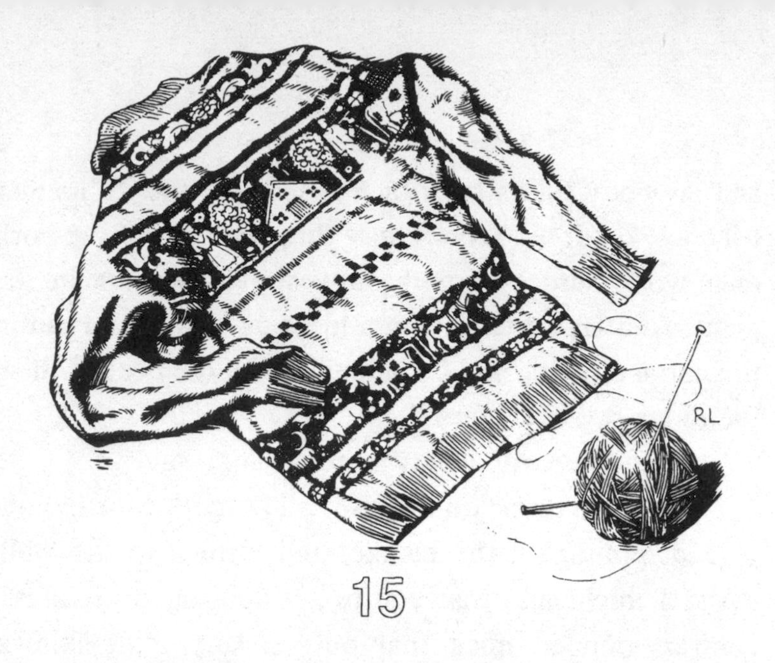

15

Two days passed, and about sunset of the third day she came. At first glance Conn mistook her for one of the waitresses from the German Village or Old Vienna, for she was wearing the same quaint, Old World costume that she had worn on the *City of Bristol*. Her pale hair was again arranged in its crown of heavy braids. She passed Conn with head held high, a slight smile on her lips. She took a seat in the farthest corner, extracted a partly finished piece of knitting from a small basket, and began to knit.

For a while Conn stood stiffly, his eyes fixed on the sky. Gradually, however, curiosity conquered pride; his gaze wandered to the far corner. There were only a few other passengers; he could watch her unobserved, for she was intent on her work. Whenever she paused it was only to look out at the sunset sky or the dark waters of the lake.

The garment she was knitting seemed to be a sweater, one of those gaily patterned sweaters that the lasses of the fishing towns back home used to make. It was dark blue, and the pattern ran across it in bands of bright color. There was one strip of gay flowers and green grass. Above it was a procession of farm animals: pigs and goats, geese, chickens, calves, horses. The topmost stripe was the broadest and most interesting of all, but it was only partly finished. There seemed to be a small white house in the center, flanked by two trees. Then there were two little figures, a man and a woman, one on either side of the house. They were completed only up to their necks, but he could see that the woman's costume was the same as Trudy's. Then came a pair of orange cows, a pair of spotted dogs, and a pair of black-and-white cats. All around were sprinkled bright little flowers.

Her hands moved like lightning; the bone needles flickered in the sun. When the car neared the summit she rose, went to the window, and stood gazing into the sunset. The thick, ringed braids blazed like a golden crown, seemed to shed an aura of golden light about her head.

"No, ma'am," Conn answered an inquiring passenger. "That's not the Palace of Fine Arts, that's the railroad station. The Fine Arts Palace is over there by the lagoon. Yes, ma'am, that's the Midway right down there. Yes'm, it's entirely safe for a lady."

By the time he had finished his explanations Trudy was again seated and busy with her knitting. At the conclusion of the trip she filed out with the other passengers as she had come in, head high, eyes straight ahead, the faintest trace of a smile.

Each day she came at the same hour, for the same trip. Always she sat in the same far-corner seat and rose, bathed in golden light, to gaze into the sunset. Always she left as she came, with no sign of recognition, head high and smiling her secret smile. The sweater progressed slowly, the girl was now completed. She had heavy braids of pale yellow hair, but the man, being taller, still lacked a head.

All week Conn simmered. In his heart, rage, shame, pride, and love battled unceasingly, now one uppermost now the other. The combat left him shaken and bewildered. Each evening he resolved furiously that he would not bear with it another day. He would go to Mr. Ferris first thing in the morning and ask to be relieved. He would take the next train to St. Louis. And each morning found him at the door of Car Number One, counting the hours till evening.

Nighttimes, at Mrs. Murphy's, Martin Brennan wisely

held his peace. Conn's return usually found him asleep or pretending sleep. He offered no comment on Conn's uneasy rest, his turnings and tossings and mutterings throughout the night.

Somehow the long week of travail passed, and the last day of the wheel's operation arrived. All day Conn alternately quivered with the thought of her arrival or sank into bottomless gloom with the fear that she might not come at all. The hour of the sunset trip came at last, and his depression deepened as the minutes sped by with no sign of her.

The weather was quite cool now; most of the attractions had closed, and there were few visitors. One pleasant-looking middle-aged lady settled herself in Car Number One. The other cars had a scattering of passengers, their guards closed and locked their doors, but Conn still waited, the door of Number One opened wide.

Suddenly she was there, her cheeks flushed pink with hurry and the brisk air. Hastily, looking neither to right nor left, she entered and took her usual seat. Conn slammed and locked the door with unnecessary violence. Trudy got out her sweater and began to knit. Her fellow passenger moved over and watched with wonder.

"Goodness gracious," she exclaimed. "That is the most beautiful sweater I have ever beheld, the very most. But so intricate, hasn't it taken just ages to do?"

"A long time," Trudy answered. "Since I have come to this country, almost a year and a half yet. But I have not worked very hard, there was no hurry."

"One couldn't hurry with anything as perfectly exquisite as that. I have never seen anything like it."

Trudy laughed. "It is the kind the girls make in the old country for their brothers and husbands."

"And sweethearts?"

"Sometimes—yes," she admitted. "But not this one. *Nein*—no."

"You seem very decided about that," the lady laughed. "The little figures are simply fascinating, I don't see how you do it. Why, my dear, the little girl looks very much like you." She examined it more closely. "Yes, of course it is. The same costume—the same golden braids. But the poor man, he hasn't any head yet. What color will *his* hair be?"

"I have not decided." Trudy shrugged indifferently. "Black, perhaps, or gray. Perhaps yellow—I have a nice friend with blond hair—like mine."

Conn got out a rag and began furiously polishing brass-work.

"Or red?" the lady suggested. "Wouldn't red be very effective?"

"No—no, not red," Trudy exclaimed. "People with red hair are cruel and cold and proud. Not red."

Her companion laughed. "Oh no, my dear, you must be mistaken. Hot-tempered yes, but not cold or cruel. Why I know several people with red hair and they—"

"No!" Trudy interrupted decisively. "They are cruel and proud—and stubborn."

The brass-polishing became more violent. Trudy laid down her work and stepped to the window, smiling at her new friend. "Let's look at the beautiful sunset, and not think about unhappy things." Silently they watched the great red globe sink into the prairie.

"Fair weather tomorrow," the friend said.

As the car slowly descended it became darker. Conn switched on the lights; Trudy resumed her knitting, working rapidly. The trip at last ended, Conn flung open the north door with his usual exit speech.

"Good-by, my dear," the lady said, rising to go, "I hope you finish your beautiful sweater soon. It will make someone very happy." Trudy, counting stitches, could not reply, but nodded and smiled a cordial farewell. She continued to knit and count.

Conn repeated his speech with emphasis, "All out, *please!* Those wishing another trip will kindly purchase tickets at the ticket office." Twitching her head impatiently, Trudy indicated a ticket stuck in the back of the next seat. Conn slammed and locked the east door, collected the ticket brusquely, and started to unlock the south door. He hesitated a moment, then put the key back in his pocket. One or two passengers approached but, seeing the door closed, moved on to Car Number Two. Conn continued his polishing, Trudy her knitting. As the car approached the summit she finished her row and gazed around speculatively.

"I think," she mused, half to herself, "I think I would like the cooking stove in the corner best. No . . . perhaps a little away. Yes . . . that would be better. Then the wood box by the door . . ." She picked up the sweater and continued her knitting. "Holsteins are better for the cheese, Oncle Otto says, but I think I would like most a Jersey cow . . . I think. Almost a pet one would be—so gentle. . . . In her stable it would be always warm . . . and on Christmas Eve at midnight she would kneel down . . ."

Her soliloquy was shattered by an anger-choked voice.

"And how would you be knowing about a cook stove, or the woodbox or a Jersey cow?" Conn demanded furiously. His bulk towered over her, dark against the evening sky.

Her eyes opened wide in seeming innocence. "From your letters," she answered calmly. "The letters that Martin Brennan gave me, the dear small man."

"He'd no right," Conn raged. "I threw them away. The little rat. I'll—"

"No you will not." She rose and faced him. "You could not hurt a little man—a cripple. A girl—yes. A girl you could hurt, but not him. Not even you."

Before her steady gaze his eyes dropped. They came to rest on the sweater lying on the seat. Suddenly he felt the blood flooding his face, pounding in his throat and ears. He pointed an unsteady finger.

"The man," he choked, "the little man—his hair—it's red!"

"Yes—red," she said. "I had no more yellow wool, or black, or white—only red. It had to be red—it was his fortune."

"And the star—over the small white house?"

"That was his fortune too."

She had been gazing out at the cool sky where now the evening star had appeared, twinkling brilliantly. Now she turned and picked up the sweater holding it before her, almost as a shield.

"Would you mind if I measure it—on you? My friend—he is almost the same size." She stretched it across his chest; she had to reach up to do it, to tilt back her head to see. Her fingers pressed it against his shoulders.

"Why, Conn . . . you are trembling. Are you cold? Oh . . . Conn . . . you are crushing your sweater." A bone needle fell to the carpet. "Now . . . you have made me drop a stitch . . . Never mind . . . Conn . . . dear . . ."

The car came gently to rest. Dimly they became aware of laughter, whoops, and a derisive chant. A half-dozen guards were lined up, peering into the brilliantly lighted car. "All out, please," they intoned. "Those wishing another ride will kindly purchase tickets at the ticket booth."

Hastily unlocking the north door, they fled, leaving the door standing wide and unlocked—the first and only time Conn had ever broken the rules.

It was almost midnight. Martin Brennan stood at the window looking across the fairgrounds, watching the great lighted wheel making its last revolution. It turned slowly, majestically; its huge glowing circle seeming to fill the sky, to make the great Fair buildings seem tiny and insignificant.

He became aware of a clatter of running feet on the stairs and of the door bursting open.

"You thieving little ragpicker you!" Conn roared.

Martin started to duck, then realized that the roar was joyous and that Conn was pounding his back affectionately. "Whisht, lad," Martin said, pointing through the window. "I'm sitting up with a dying friend." Conn fell silent and they both watched as the giant wheel at last came to its final stop. Across the grounds there floated

RL

the thin sweet keening of Little Betsy's whistle. Some minutes it wailed, then reluctantly died away.

As its last notes ceased, the great circle of light suddenly disappeared, leaving nothing but blackness. Conn rubbed his eyes and looked again; there was nothing. It was as though the wheel had never existed.

"Martin," Conn asked, with a sheepish grin. "Will you be best man for me?"

Martin, bursting with pleasure and embarrassment, colored and plucked at his nails. "Now wouldn't it be an odd and contradictory sight," he said, "a little twisty thing the like of me being called the best man, with that great giant of an Uncle Patrick of yours standing by?"

"It will not," Conn said. "Uncle Patrick may be the biggest but he's not the best, and we'll be having nothing but the best, so make up your mind to it."

16

A few weeks later Conn came walking down the hill from the Zillheimer Model Creamery. If he was going to learn the cheese business, Uncle Otto said, the place to begin was at the bottom, and the bottom was the cow barns and the creamery. Conn liked it; he liked cows anyway, he liked the excessive cleanliness and order of the creamery, he liked the smell and the look of the huge vats of foaming milk and cream. And, being a smart young man, he was learning with that same rapidity that had so astonished Uncle Michael.

Now he stopped at their own small barn to look in on their own small cow, a beautiful little Jersey that he had purchased from his own savings. Trudy, he could see, had already done the milking, so he tossed the cow a little more hay, slapped her flank, and continued on down the hill toward home.

Home was a neat little farmhouse much like the one that graced his new sweater, that sweater so beautiful and so dear that it was only worn on extra special occasions. The house, the barn, and their surrounding acres had been Uncle Otto's wedding present. Conn liked the location; the hill behind them shut off the view of the big barns, the distant creamery, and Uncle Otto's great sprawling stone house. Here they were all alone.

Trudy came running to meet him, a heavy shawl flung over her shoulders, for the evening was crisply cold. His dog, a large, nondescript spotted hound, gamboled and bellowed a greeting. It was their favorite spot to meet, for here they could watch the sun set behind the hill, and a bit later Aunt Honora's star would appear directly over the house, just as it did on the sweater.

This evening as they waited they suddenly became aware of a commotion in the roadway, and a moment later two teams of the great dappled Zillheimer horses swung in through the gate hauling a long, low-swung dray. On the dray was perched a dark bulk of some sort—Conn couldn't tell what. The driver clucked; the steaming teams strained and emerged into the open.

"Glory be!" shouted Conn. "It's Car Number One!"

The reflected sunset set all the windows aflame, and

sparkled on the glittering brasswork. Conn and Trudy, breathless with excitement, raced down the hill to meet it, to peer in the windows, to handle its shining door-knobs, to trace with eager fingers the polished brass figure 1 on the door.

"Where at would you want this put, Conn?" the grinning driver asked. Conn hadn't the faintest idea, but Trudy had already chosen the spot, a slight knoll not far from the house. So the horses once more leaned into their collars and the lumbering load slowly moved to its final resting place.

As the driver unhitched his horses he paused and drew a small package from his pocket. "This here belongs with it," he said. "The freight agent gave it to me."

The package contained a little box of polished wood lined with velvet. On the velvet lay the shining brass key to Car Number One and a card from Mr. and Mrs. Ferris wishing them many years of happiness.

"The dear, kind people," Trudy said, slipping the key into the lock. She smiled teasingly at Conn over her shoulder.

"Do you still want to move into it?" she asked.

Conn laughed contentedly. "I don't think so—now," he said. "I'm suited where I am. But I'm thinking it will make a grand playhouse for your George Washington Ferris Martin Patrick Kilroy."

ABOUT THE AUTHOR

Robert Lawson (1892–1957) is the only author-illustrator to win both the Caldecott Medal and Newbery Medal for excellence in children's illustration and literature. His evocative characters and meticulous line drawings graced such classic children's books as *The Story of Ferdinand, Mr. Popper's Penguins,* and his Newbery Medal–winning *Rabbit Hill.* The Caldecott Medal was awarded to him for *They Were Strong and Good;* having previously received Caldecott Honors for *Wee Gillis* and *Four and Twenty Blackbirds.* He wrote and illustrated eighteen books for children during his career, most from his Westport, Connecticut, estate, Rabbit Hill. *The Great Wheel,* a 1958 Newbery Honor Book, was his last.

His work continues to inspire illustrators, writers, and readers throughout the field of children's literature.